Aesop

Three Hundred and Fifty AEsop's Fables

Aesop

Three Hundred and Fifty AEsop's Fables

ISBN/EAN: 9783744788601

Printed in Europe, USA, Canada, Australia, Japan

Cover: Foto ©Andreas Hilbeck / pixelio.de

More available books at **www.hansebooks.com**

ÆSOP'S FABLES.

Frontispiece.

THREE HUNDRED AND FIFTY

ÆSOP'S FABLES,

LITERALLY TRANSLATED FROM THE GREEK.

BY THE

REV. GEO. FYLER TOWNSEND, M. A.

———

With One Hundred and Fourteen Illustrations, Designed by Harrison Weir, and Engraved by J. Greenaway.

———

CHICAGO:
BELFORD, CLARKE & CO.,
1882.

PREFACE.

THE TALE, the Parable, and the Fable are all common and popular modes of conveying instruction.   Each is distinguished by its own special characteristics. The Tale consists simply in the narration of a story either founded on facts, or created solely by the imagination, and not necessarily associated with the teaching of any moral lesson. The Parable is the designed use of language purposely intended to convey a hidden and secret meaning other than that contained in the words themselves; and which may or may not bear a special reference to the hearer, or reader. The Fable partly agrees with, and partly differs from both of these. It will contain, like the Tale, a short but real narrative; it will seek, like the Parable, to convey a hidden meaning, and that not so much by the use of language, as by the skilful introduction of fictitious characters; and yet unlike to either Tale or Parable, it will ever keep in view, as its high prerogative, and inseparable attribute, the great purpose of instruction, and will necessarily seek to inculcate some moral maxim, social duty, or political truth. The true Fable, if it rise to its high requirements, ever aims at one great end and purpose —the representation of human motive, and the improvement of human conduct, and yet it so conceals its design under the disguise of fictitious characters, by clothing with speech the animals of the field, the birds of the air, the trees of the wood, or the beasts of the forest, that the reader shall receive advice without perceiving the presence of the adviser. Thus the superiority of the counselor, which often renders counsel unpalatable, is kept out of view, and the lesson comes with the greater acceptance when the reader is led, unconsciously to himself, to have his sympathies enlisted in behalf of what is pure, honorable, and praiseworthy, and to have his indignation excited against what is low, ignoble, and unworthy. The true fabulist, therefore, discharges a most important function. He is neither a narrator, nor an allegorist. He is a great teacher, a corrector of morals, a censor of vice, and a commender of virtue. In this consists the superiority of the Fable over the Tale or the Parable. The fabulist is to create a laugh, but yet, under a merry guise, to convey instruction. Phædrus, the great imitator of Æsop, plainly indicates this double purpose to be the true office of the writer of fables.

> Duplex libelli dos est: quod risum movet,
> Et quod prudenti vitam consilio monet.

The continual observance of this twofold aim creates the charm, and accounts for the universal favor, of the fables of Æsop. "The fable," says Professor K. O. Mueller, "originated in Greece in an intentional travestie of human affairs. The 'ainos,' as its name denotes, is an admonition, or rather a reproof, veiled, either from fear of an excess of frankness, or from a love of fun and jest, beneath the fiction of an occurrence happening among beasts; and wherever we have any ancient and authentic account of the Æsopian fables, we find it to be the same." *

The construction of a fable involves a minute attention to (1), the narration itself; (2), the deduction of the moral; and (3), a careful maintenance of the individual characteristics of the fictitious personages introduced into it. The narration should relate to one simple action, consistent with itself, and neither be overladen with a multiplicity of details,

---

* A History of the Literature of Ancient Greece, by K. O. Mueller. Vol. I., p. 191. London, Parker, 1858.

nor distracted by a variety of circumstances. The moral or lesson should be so plain, and so intimately interwoven with, and so necessarily dependent on, the narration, that every reader should be compelled to give to it the same undeniable interpretation. The introduction of the animals or fictitious characters should be marked with an unexceptionable care and attention to their natural attributes, and to the qualities attributed to them by universal popular consent. The Fox should be always cunning, the Hare timid, the Lion bold, the Wolf cruel, the Bull strong, the Horse proud, and the Ass patient. Many of these fables are characterized by the strictest observance of these rules. They are occupied with one short narrative, from which the moral naturally flows, and with which it is intimately associated. "'Tis the simple manner," says Dodsley,* "in which the morals of Æsop are interwoven with his fables that distinguishes him, and gives him the preference over all other mythologists. His 'Mountain delivered of a Mouse,' produces the moral of his fable in ridicule of pompous pretenders; and his Crow, when she drops her cheese, lets fall, as it were by accident, the strongest admonition against the power of

* Select Fables of Æsop, and other Fabulists. In three books, translated by Robert Dodsley, accompanied with a selection of notes, and an Essay on Fable. Birmingham, 1811. P. 60.

flattery. There is no need of a separate sentence to explain it; no possibility of impressing it deeper, by that load we too often see of accumulated reflec-tions."† An equal amount of praise is due for the consistency with which the characters of the ani-mals, fictitiously introduced, are marked. While they are made to depict the motives and passions of men, they retain, in an eminent degree, their own special features of craft or counsel, of cowardice or courage, of generosity or rapacity.

These terms of praise, it must be confessed, can-not be bestowed on all the fables in this collection. Many of them lack that unity of design, that close connection of the moral with the narrative, that wise choice in the introduction of the animals, which constitute the charm and excellency of true Æsopian

---

† Some of these fables had, no doubt, in the first instance, a primary and private interpretation. On the first occasion of their being composed they were intended to refer to some passing event, or to some individual acts of wrong-doing. Thus, the fables of the "Eagle and the Fox" (p. 219), of the "Fox and Monkey" (p. 80), are supposed to have been written by Archilo-chus, to avenge the injuries done him by Lycambes. So also the fables of the "Swollen Fox" (p. 132), of the "Frogs asking a King" (p. 65), were spoken by Æsop for the immediate purpose of reconciling the inhabitants of Samos and Athens, to their respective rulers, Periander and Pisistratus; while the fable of the "Horse and Stag" was composed to caution the inhab-itants of Himera against granting a body-guard to Phalaris. In a similar manner, the fable from Phædrus, the "Marriage of the Sun," is supposed to have reference to the contemplated union of Livia, the daughter of Drusus, with Sejanus the favorite, and minister of Trajan. These fables, how-ever, though thus originating in special events, and designed at first to meet special circumstances, are so admirably constructed as to be fraught with lessons of general utility, and of universal application.

fable. This inferiority of some to others is suffi-
ciently accounted for in the history of the origin and
descent of these fables. The great bulk of them are
not the immediate work of Æsop. Many are obtained
from ancient authors prior to the time in which he
lived. Thus the fable of the "Hawk and the Nightingale" is related by Hesiod;* the "Eagle wounded
by an Arrow, winged with its own Feathers," by
Æschylus;† the "Fox avenging his wrongs on the
Eagle," by Archilochus. ‡ Many of them again are
of later origin, and are to be traced to the monks of
the middle ages: and yet this collection, though thus
made up of fables both earlier and later than the
era of Æsop, rightfully bears his name, because he
composed so large a number (all framed in the same
mould, and conformed to the same fashion, and
stamped with the same lineaments, image, and
superscription) as to secure to himself the right to
be considered the father of Greek fables, and the
founder of this class of writing, which has ever
since borne his name, and has secured for him,

---

* Hesiod. Opera et dies, verse 202.

† Æschylus. Fragment of the Myrmidons. Æschylus speaks of this fable as existing before his day. See Scholiast on the Aves of Aristophanes, line 808.

‡ Fragment, 38, ed. Gaisford. See also Mueller's History of the Literature of Ancient Greece, vol. I., pp. 190-193.

through all succeeding ages, the position of the first of moralists.*

The fables were in the first instance only narrated by Æsop, and for a long time were handed down by the uncertain channel of oral tradition. Socrates is mentioned by Plato † as having employed his time while in prison, awaiting the return of the sacred ship from Delphos which was to be the signal of his death, in turning some of these fables into verse, but he thus versified only such as he remembered. Demetrius Phalereus, a philosopher at Athens about 300 B.C., is said to have made the first collection of these fables. Phædrus, a slave by birth or by subsequent misfortunes, and admitted by Augustus to the honors of a freedman, imitated many of these fables in Latin iambics about the commencement of the Christian era. Aphthonius, a rhetorician of Antioch, A.C. 315, wrote a treatise on, and converted into Latin prose, some of these fables. This translation is the the more worthy of notice, as it illustrates a custom

---

* M. Bayle has well put this in his account of Æsop. "Il n'y a point d'apparence que les fables qui portent aujourd'hui son nom soient les mêmes qu'il avait faites; elles viennent bien de lui pour la plupart, quant à la matière et la pensée; mais les paroles sont d'un autre." And again, "C'est donc à Hésiode, que j'aimerais mieux attribuer la gloire de l'invention; mais sans doute il laissa la chose très imparfaite. Esope la perfectionne si heureusement, qu'on l'a regarde comme le vrai père de cette sorte de production."— Bayle, Dictionnaire Historique.

† Plato in Phædone.

of common use, both in these and in later times. The rhetoricians and philosophers were accustomed to give the Fables of Æsop as an exercise to their scholars, not only inviting them to discuss the moral of the tale, but also to practice and to perfect themselves thereby in style and rules of grammar, by making for themselves new and various versions of the fables. Ausonius,* the friend of the Emperor Valentinian, and the latest poet of eminence in the Western Empire, has handed down some of these fables in verse, which Julianus Titianus, a contemporary writer of no great name, translated into prose. Avienus, also, a contemporary of Ausonius, put some of these fables into Latin elegiacs, which are given by Nevelet (in a book we shall refer to hereafter), and are occasionally incorporated with the editions of Phædrus.

Seven centuries elapsed before the next notice is found of the Fables of Æsop. During this long period these fables seem to have suffered an eclipse, to have disappeared and to have been forgotten; and it

---

*Apologos en! misit tibi
Ab usque Rheni limite
Ausonius nomen Italum
Præceptor Augusti tui
Æsopiam trimetriam;
Quam vertit exili stylo
Pedestre concinnans opus
Fandi Titianus artifex.
"Ausonii Epistolæ," xvi. 75-80.

is at the commencement of the fourteenth century, when the Byzantine emperors were the great patrons of learning, and amidst the splendors of an Asiatic court, that we next find honors paid to the name and memory of Æsop. Maximus Planudes, a learned monk of Constantinople, made' a collection of about a hundred and fifty of these fables. Little is known of his history. Planudes, however, was no mere recluse, shut up in his monastery. He took an active part in public affairs. In 1327 A.D. he was sent on a diplomatic mission to Venice by the Emperor Andronicus the Elder. This brought him into immediate contact with the Western Patriarch, whose interests he henceforth advocated with so much zeal as to bring on him suspicion and persecution from the rulers of the Eastern Church. Planudes has been exposed to a two-fold accusation. He is charged on the one hand with having had before him a copy of Babrias (to whom we shall have occasion to refer at greater length in the end of this Preface), and to have had the bad taste " to transpose," or to turn his poetical version into prose: and he is asserted, on the other hand, never to have seen the Fables of Æsop at all, but to have himself invented and made the fables which he palmed off under the name of the famous Greek fabulist. The truth lies between these two extremes.   Planudes may have invented some few fables, or have inserted some that were current in his day; but there is an abundance of unanswerable internal evidence to prove that he had an acquaintance with the veritable Fables of Æsop, although the versions he had access to were probably corrupt, as contained in the various translations and disquisitional exercises of the rhetoricians and philosophers.   His collection is interesting and important, not only as the parent source or foundation of the earlier printed versions of Æsop, but as the direct channel of attracting to these fables the attention of the learned.

The eventual re-introduction, however, of these Fables of Æsop to their high place in the general literature of Christendom, is to be looked for in the West rather than in the East.   The calamities gradually thickening round the Eastern Empire, and the fall of Constantinople, 1453 A.D. combined with other events to promote the rapid restoration of learning in Italy; and with that recovery of learning the revival of an interest in the Fables of Æsop is closely identified.   These fables, indeed, were among the first writings of an earlier antiquity that attracted attention.   They took their place beside the Holy Scriptures and the ancient classic authors, in the minds of the great students of that day.   Lorenzo

Valla, one of the most famous promoters of Italian learning, not only translated into Latin the Iliad of Homer and the Histories of Herodotus and Thucydides, but also the Fables of Æsop.

These fables, again, were among the books brought into an extended circulation by the agency of the printing press. Bonus Accursius, as early as 1475-1480, printed the collection of these fables, made by Planudes, which, within five years afterwards, Caxton translated into English, and printed at his press in Westminster Abbey, 1485.* It must be mentioned also that the learning of this age has left permanent traces of its influence on these fables,† by causing the interpolation with them of some of those amusing

---

* Both these publications are in the British Museum, and are placed in the library in cases under glass, for the inspection of the curious.

† Fables may possibly have been not entirely unknown to the mediæval scholars. There are two celebrated works which might by some be classed amongst works of this description. The one is the "Speculum Sapientiæ," attributed to St. Cyril, Archbishop of Jerusalem, but of a considerably later origin, and existing only in Latin. It is divided into four books, and consists of long conversations conducted by fictitious characters under the figures of the beasts of the field and forest, and aimed at the rebuke of particular classes of men, the boastful, the proud, the luxurious, the wrathful, etc. None of the stories are precisely those of Æsop, and none have the concinnity, terseness, and unmistakable deduction of the lesson intended to be taught by the fable, so conspicuous in the great Greek fabulist. The exact title of the book is this: "Speculum Sapientiæ, B. Cyrilli Episcopi: alias quadripartitus apologeticus vocatus, in cujus quidem proverbiis omnis et totius sapientiæ speculum claret et feliciter incipit." The other is a larger work in two volumes, published in the fourteenth century by Cæsar Heisterbach, a Cistercian monk, under the title of "Dialogus Miraculorum," reprinted in 1851. This work consists of conversations in which many stories are interwoven on all kinds of subjects. It has no correspondence with the pure Æsopian fable.

stories which were so frequently introduced into the public discourses of the great preachers of those days, and of which specimens are yet to be found in the extant sermons of Jean Raulin, Meffreth, and Gabriel Barlette.* The publication of this era which most probably has influenced these fables, is the "Liber Facetiarum,"† a book consisting of a hundred jests and stories, by the celebrated Poggio Bracciolini, published A.D. 1471, from which the two fables of the "Miller, his Son, and the Ass," p. 133, and the "Fox and the Woodcutter," p. 125, are undoubtedly selected.

The knowledge of these fables rapidly spread from Italy into Germany, and their popularity was increased by the favor and sanction given to them by the great fathers of the Reformation, who frequently used them as vehicles for satire and protest against the tricks and abuses of the Romish ecclesiastics. The zealous and renowned Camerarius, who took an active part in the preparation of the confession of Augsburgh, found time, amidst his numerous avocations, to prepare a version for the students in the university of Tübingen, in which he was a professor.

---

* Post-mediæval Preachers, by S. Baring-Gould. Rivingtons, 1865.

† For an account of this work see the Life of Poggio Bracciolini, by the Rev. William Shepherd. Liverpool. 1801.

Martin Luther translated twenty of these fables, and was urged by Melancthon to complete the whole; while Gottfried Arnold, the celebrated Lutheran theologian, and librarian to Frederick I., king of Prussia, mentions that the great Reformer valued the Fables of Æsop next after the Holy Scriptures. In 1546 A.D. the second printed edition of the collection of the Fables made by Planudes, was issued from the printing-press of Robert Stephens, in which were inserted some additional fables from a MS. in the Bibliothêque du Roy at Paris.

The greatest advance, however, towards a re-introduction of the Fables of Æsop to a place in the literature of the world, was made in the early part of the seventeenth century. In the year 1610, a learned Swiss, Isaac Nicholas Nevelet, sent forth the third printed edition of these fables, in a work entitled " Mythologia Æsopica." This was a noble effort to do honor to the great fabulist, and was the most perfect collection of Æsopian fables ever yet published. It consisted, in addition to the collection of fables given by Planudes and reprinted in the various earlier editions, of one hundred and thirty-six new fables (never before published) from MSS. in the Library of the Vatican, of forty fables attributed to Aphthonius, and of forty-three from Babrias. It also contained the Latin versions of the same fables by Phædrus, Avienus, and other authors. This volume of Nevelet forms a complete "Corpus Fabularum Æsopicarum;" and to his labors Æsop owes his restoration to universal favor as one of the wise moralists and great teachers of mankind. During the interval of three centuries which has elapsed since the publication of this volume of Nevelet's, no book, with the exception of the Holy Scriptures, has had a wider circulation than Æsop's Fables. They have been translated into the greater number of the languages both of Europe and of the East, and have been read, and will be read, for generations, alike by Jew, Heathen, Mohammedan, and Christian. They are, at the present time, not only engrafted into the literature of the civilized world, but are familiar as household words in the common intercourse and daily conversation of the inhabitants of all countries.

This collection of Nevelet's is the great culminating point in the history of the revival of the fame and reputation of Æsopian Fables. It is remarkable, also, as containing in its preface the germ of an idea, which has been since proved to have been correct by a strange chain of circumstances. Nevelet intimates an opinion, that a writer named Babrias would be found to be the veritable author of the existing

form of Æsopian Fables. This intimation has since
given rise to a series of inquiries, the knowledge of
which is necessary, in the present day, to a full understanding of the true position of Æsop in connection with the writings that bear his name.

The history of Babrias is so strange and interesting, that it might not unfitly be enumerated among
the curiosities of literature. He is generally supposed to have been a Greek of Asia Minor, of one of
the Ionic Colonies, but the exact period in which he
lived and wrote is yet unsettled. He is placed, by
one critic,* as far back as the institution of the
Achaian League, B.C. 250, by another as late as the
Emperor Severus, who died A.D. 235; while others
make him a contemporary with Phædrus in the time
of Augustus. At whatever time he wrote his version of Æsop, by some strange accident it seems to
have entirely disappeared, and to have been lost
sight of. His name is mentioned by Avienus; by
Suidas, a celebrated critic, at the close of the elev-
enth century, who gives in his lexicon several iso-
lated verses of his version of the fables; and by John
Tzetzes, a grammarian and poet of Constantinople,
who lived during the latter half of the twelfth cen-

---

* Professor Theodore Bergh. See Classical Museum, No. viii. July, 1849.

tury. Nevelet, in the preface to the volume which we have described, points out that the Fables of Planudes could not be the work of Æsop, as they contain a reference in two places to "Holy monks," and give a verse from the Epistle of St. James as an "Epimith" to one of the fables, and suggests Babrias as their author. Francis Vavassor,* a learned French jesuit, entered at greater length on this subject, and produced further proofs from internal evidence, from the use of the word Piræus in describing the harbor of Athens, a name which was not given till two hundred years after Æsop, and from the introduction of other modern words, that many of these fables must have been at least committed to writing posterior to the time of Æsop, and more boldly suggests Babrias as their author or collector.† These various references to Babrias induced Dr. Richard Bentley, at the close of the seventeenth century, to examine more minutely the existing versions of Æsop's Fables,

---

* Vavassor's treatise, entitled "De Ludicra Dictione" was written A.D. 1658, at the request of the celebrated M. Balzac (though published after his death), for the purpose of showing that the burlesque style of writing adopted by Scarron and D'Assouci, and at that time so popular in France, had no sanction from the ancient classic writers.—"Francisci Vavassoris opera omnia." Amsterdam, 1709.

† The claims of Babrias also found a warm advocate in the learned Frenchman, M. Bayle, who, in his admirable Dictionary, ("Dictionnaire Historique et Critique de Pierre Bayle." Paris, 1820,) gives additional arguments in confirmation of the opinions of his learned predecessors, Nevelet and Vavassor.

and he maintained that many of them could, with a
slight change of words, be resolved into the Scazonic* iambics, in which Babrias is known to have
written: and, with a greater freedom than the evidence then justified, he put forth, in behalf of Babrias,
a claim to the exclusive authorship of these fables.
Such a seemingly extravagant theory, thus roundly
asserted, excited much opposition. Dr. Bentley† met
with an able antagonist in a member of the University of Oxford, the Hon. Mr. Charles Boyle,‡ afterwards Earl of Orrery. Their letters and disputations
on this subject, enlivened on both sides with much
wit and learning, will ever bear a conspicuous place
in the literary history of the seventeenth century.
The arguments of Dr. Bentley were yet further defended a few years later by Mr. Thomas Tyrwhitt, a
well-read scholar, who gave up high civil distinc-
tions that he might devote himself the more unreserv-
edly to literary pursuits. Mr. Tyrwhitt published,
A.D. 1776, a Dissertation on Babrias, and a collec-

---

* Scazonic, or halting, iambics; a choliambic (a lame, halting iambic) differs from the iambic Senarius in always having a spondee or trochee for its
last foot; the fifth foot, to avoid shortness of metre, being generally an
iambic. See Fables of Babrias, translated by Rev. James Davies. Lock-
wood, 1860. Preface, p. 27.

† See Dr. Bentley's Dissertations upon the Epistles of Phalaris.

‡ Dr. Bentley's Dissertations on the Epistles of Phalaris, and Fables of
Æsop examined. By the Honorable Charles Boyle.

tion of his fables in choliambic metre, found in a MS. in the Bodleian Library at Oxford. Francesco de Furia, a learned Italian, contributed further testimony to the correctness of the supposition that Babrias had made a veritable collection of fables by printing from a MS. contained in the Vatican library several fables never before published. In the year 1844, however, new and unexpected light was thrown upon this subject. A veritable copy of Babrias was found in a manner as singular as were the MSS. of Quinctilian's Institutes, and of Cicero's Orations by Poggio in the monastery of St. Gall A.D. 1416. M. Menoïdes, at the suggestion of M. Villemain, Minister of Public Instruction to King Louis Philippe, had been entrusted with a commission to search for ancient MSS., and in carrying out his instructions he found a MS. at the convent of St. Laura, on Mount Athos, which proved to be a copy of the long suspected and wished-for choliambic version of Babrias. This MS. was found to be divided into two books, the one containing one hundred and twenty-five, and the other ninety-five fables. This discovery attracted very general attention, not only as confirming, in a singular manner, the conjectures so boldly made by a long chain of critics, but as bringing to light valuable literary treasures tending to establish the reputation, and to confirm the antiquity and authenticity of the great mass of Æsopian Fable. The Fables thus recovered were soon published. They found a most worthy editor in the late distinguished Sir George Cornewall Lewis, and a translator equally qualified for his task, in the Reverend James Davies, M.A., sometime a scholar of Lincoln College, Oxford, and himself a relation of their English editor. Thus, after an eclipse of many centuries, Babrias shines out as the earliest, and most reliable collector of veritable Æsopian Fables.

Having thus given a complete synopsis of the origin, descent, and history of these fables, it only remains to explain the reasons which have induced the Publishers to prepare a new edition of Æsop, and to state the grounds on which they hope to establish a claim for support and public approval in their undertaking. They boldly assert that the new light thrown upon these fables by the discovery of the metrical version by Babrias, renders a new translation an inevitable necessity. The two chief existing English versions of Æsop are those by Archdeacon Croxall, and by the late Rev. Thomas James, canon of Peterborough. The first of these deviates so very far from the text, that it degenerates into a parody. The fables are so padded, diluted, and altered, as to give very little idea to the reader either of the terseness or the meaning of the original. The second of these is an improvement on its predecessor, but Mr. James, either out of compliance with the wishes of the publishers, or in condescension to the taste prevalent some twenty years ago, has so freely introduced as the point of the fable conventional English sayings which are not sanctioned by the Greek, and which in many instances are scarcely equivalent to it, that his version frequently approaches a paraphrase rather than a translation.

The Publishers therefore ground their first claim for public approval on the necessity for a new translation. They trust further that their present work will have met that necessity in a satisfactory manner. They have sought to give as nearly a literal translation as possible of the Greek text; and they hope that if the reader should miss the smoothness and thoroughly English tone which characterized the previous version of these fables, he will be more than repaid, by gaining a nearer approach to the spirit, thoughts, and (in some cases) to the epigrammatic terseness of the original. The publishers trust to vindicate, on another ground, their claims to a share of public patronage. They have inserted an hundred new fables, and they have the satisfaction of knowing that this edition, on which they have spared no pains nor cost, will afford a larger choice, and greater variety, to the numerous and increasing circle of the admirers of Æsopian Fables. Whatever be the result of their labors, they will be content to have contributed towards promoting a wider acquaintance with fables, the wisdom, excellency, and wonderful suitableness of which to every condition of humanity has been attested and confirmed by the experience of so many generations; and, which, in all ages amidst the ever changing fluctuations of human opinion, are adapted alike to amuse the young, and to instruct the thoughtful, and are well fitted to teach all who study them lessons useful for their guidance in every position of political, social, civil, or domestic life.

The Editor must claim the privilege of adding a few words on a matter personal to himself. He has already within the last few months been connected with one edition of Æsop, and it may seem strange that he should be willing to undertake the superintendence of another. His answer is, that the two works on which he has been engaged were totally distinct, and entirely independent of each other. The first was a request to furnish new morals and applications to a definite number of fables; the other was a commission to add a large number of additional

fables and to make a wholly new translation. The
necessity of a new and improved translation the
Editor then recognized, and would have willingly
undertaken. It was a wish he had much at heart,
and when the proposal was voluntarily made to him
by the present Publishers to undertake the task of
a new translation of an enlarged number of Æsop's
Fables, he saw no reason for refusing the offer because of his prior discharge of a totally different design; and he resolved to comply with the request
submitted to him, and to do his best toward the at-
tainment of so desirable an object as a purer translation, and more literal rendering of fables so justly
celebrated.

The following are the sources from which the present translation has been prepared:

Babrii Fabulæ Æsopeæ. George Cornewall Lewis. Oxford, 1846.

Babrii Fabulæ Æsopeæ. E codice manuscripto partem secundam edidit.
George Cornewall Lewis. London: Parker, 1857.

Mythologica Æsopica. Opera et studia Isaaci Nicholai Neveleti. Frank-
fort, 1610.

Fabulæ Æsopiacæ, quales ante Planudem ferebantur cum et studio
Francisci de Furia. Lipsiæ, 1810.

Ex recognitione Caroli Halmii. Lipsiæ, 1851.

Phaedri Fabulæ Esopiæ. Delphin Classics. 1832.

THE LIFE OF ÆSOP.

THE knowledge of the Egyptians was concealed in hieroglyphics and other mysterious characters; that of the Grecians in symbols and emblematical allusions; but Æsop, having penetrated through the veil they had thrown over her, brought all their mysteries to light, and wrapped them up in fables. His life, as recorded by Planudes and other writers of antiquity, is here faithfully presented to the public.

He was born at Ammonius, in Phrygia the Greater; a town in itself obscure, though, from its being the birthplace of Æsop, might successfully have entered into competition as a rival with those cities that with a noble emulation contended for the birth of Homer.

All agree that his person was uncommonly deformed, insomuch that the Thersites of Homer seems to be but an imperfect transcript of him. His head was long, nose flat, lips thick and pendent, a hump back, and complexion dark, from which he contracted his name (Æsopus being the same with Æthiops), large belly, and bow legs; but his greatest infirmity was, that his speech was slow, inarticulate, and very obscure. Such was the person of Æsop. But, as Nature often sets the most refulgent gems where they would be least expected, so she endowed this extraordinary man with an accomplished mind, capable of the most sublime and elevated ideas. His station in life also, as well as his person, was mean and contemptible; the former part of which was spent in the most abject poverty, and the latter in slavery, till a few years before his death.

His first master (under whose dominion he then groaned), finding him incapable of any domestic business, employed him in the field, where, not long after, he gave the first testimony of his ingenuity. It happened one day, when his master was walking in the field, that a laborer presented him with some delicious figs; which he immediately gave to the care of Agathopodus (another of his servants) till he returned from the bath. But he, in league with his fellow-servant, agreed to eat them, and lay the guilt upon Æsop. When the master returned, they loudly accused Æsop of eating the figs. The master, enraged, sent for Æsop, and asked him what could induce him to eat the figs he had ordered to be reserved? Not answering readily in his defence, he was ordered to be punished. But, falling at his master's feet, he implored him to suspend the punishment. In which interval he ran and fetched some warm water, and drank it; then, putting his finger down his throat, he caused the water to return, for he had eaten nothing that day. He then requested that his accusers might be ordered to do the same; which, his master approving, they were told to do; and the consequence was, that Æsop s innocence was apparent, and his enemies were given to the punishment they justly deserved.

The day following his master returned to the city, and Æsop was remanded to his labor; when he met two priests of Diana who had lost their way. They commanded him, in the name of Jove, to direct them into the most regular track; which he not only performed, but refreshed them with meat; for which kindness he gained their good wishes, as well as their prayers.

Æsop, returning to his task, oppressed with care and labor, lay down to sleep; and in a dream beheld Fortune standing by him, gratifying him with volubility of language, and the ability of wrapping up his ideas in the form of apologues. Immediately starting up, he exclaimed, "O wonderful! in what a charming trance have I been ; for, behold, I speak fluently, and can register each creature by its name. This certainly is the reward of my compliance and kindness to the strangers." Overjoyed, he went to his labor. Having committed some fault, Zenas (overseer of the field) struck him. — "You are always," said Æsop, "punishing him that offends you not. If my master knew it, he would, no doubt, revenge these stripes." Zenas, filled with enmity, and astonished to hear him speak fluently, resolved (by way of prevention, lest he should be discharged as an unjust steward,) to accuse him to his master; whom, not long after, he accosted, desiring the gods to protect him. Upon which his master inquired, what it was that discomposed him? Zenas replied, "Something wonderful in the field." The master asked, what the wonder could be? He answered, " Æsop, who was thought dumb, has now found utterance and elocution." His master observed, " This will be ruinous to thee, in whose estimation he was reputed a monster." Zenas rejoined, "What he hath spitefully spoken against me I should have buried in silence ; but against you and the gods he hath uttered intolerable curses." This so incensed his master, that he ordered him to be sold for a slave as a recompense for his ingratitude and impiety.

No sooner had Zenas got Æsop in his power than he informed him how he was to be disposed of. To whom he replied, "Do your pleasure." Shortly after which a merchant, coming to buy cattle, met Zenas; who told him, that though he had no cattle, he had a man slave to sell. The merchant, hearing this, desired to see him. Æsop being introduced, he burst into laughter, saying, "Had I not been convinced by his voice, I should have taken him for a blown bladder. Why did you draw me aside to shock my eyes with such a deformed monster?" As he departed, Æsop desired him to stop. The merchant replied, "Be gone, you filthy cur." Æsop then requested to know for what cause he came thither. He replied, "To buy something of value, not such a worthless thing as thou art." Æsop then pressed him to buy him, promising he should find him worth his money. The merchant desired him to explain himself. "Have you at home," said Æsop, "any testy children?—I shall supply the place of bugbear, to terrify them into silence." Zenas was then asked, what he would take for that uncouth creature? "Three half-pence," said he. The merchant paid the price, observing that with nothing he had bought nothing.

When they were come near home, two of the merchant's children, seeing Æsop, testified their fear of him by crying. "Now, sir," said Æsop, "you see the effect of my promise." As they went into the house the merchant, smiling, commanded Æsop to salute his fellow-servants; who, when they beheld his deformity, exclaimed "What could induce my master to bring such a wretch into his family!"

Shortly after this the merchant ordered all things to be got ready for an intended journey into Asia. When they were assigning to each servant his proportion of burden, Æsop desired (it being his first time) that he might have the lightest. His request being granted, he took up the basket of bread; at which the other slaves laughed, considering that burden enough for two. But when dinner-time approached, Æsop, (who had with great difficulty sustained his load) was commanded to set it down, and distribute an equal share of the bread to the other slaves. His load being thus diminished one half, he pursued his journey with pleasure. At supper-time he was again ordered to distribute of his load; after which (the basket being emptied) the next morning he led the van, and obliged those, who before had treated him with contempt, to applaud his ingenuity.

Being arrived at Ephesus, and having sold divers of his slaves to good advantage, the merchant was persuaded to sail with the last three to Samos; namely, Cantor, a native of Cappadocia, and Grammaticus, born in Lydia; two persons of large dimensions; and Æsop, whose character was before described. Now, in order that he might the better sell the two former, he dressed them in new clothes; but (supposing that no art could improve him) he clothed Æsop in sackcloth, which exposed him as well to derision as to sale. Among those who came to buy was Xanthus, an eminent philosopher of Samos, attended with his scholars; who, having viewed the slaves, and seeing Æsop placed in the midst, supposed he was set there that the other two might appear to a greater advantage.

The philosopher first addressed himself to Cantor, demanding what he could perform. "All things." said he. Xanthus then demanded what price was set upon him. The merchant replied, "A thousand half-pence." Xanthus, displeased at the price, went to the other, and asked him what he could do. He also replied, "All things." The philosopher then asked the price of Grammaticus. He was told, "three thousand half-pence." Xanthus, thinking this also too much, declared he would buy no servants that were rated at so high a price. Upon which the scholars suggested to Xanthus to buy Æsop, saying they would pay for him. "'Tis not fit," said Xanthus, "that I should buy him, and you make good the payment. Besides, my wife would be much displeased to have such a misshapen person to wait upon her." The scholars replied, "We are not always obliged to comply with the desires of a woman; therefore let us examine this deformed creature." Xanthus, turning to Æsop, bid him be comforted. "Was I ever sad?" replied Æsop. "Of what place are you a native?" said the philosopher. "I am a negro," said Æsop. "I do not ask you that, but where you were born." Æsop answered, "Of my mother." "Neither did I ask that," said Xanthus, "but what place were you born in?" "My mother never informed me whether above or below." "What can you perform?" "Nothing," replied Æsop; "the two former having told you they can do all things, there remains nothing for me to do." "Are you willing," said Xanthus, "that I should buy you?" "You ought," answered

Æsop, "to judge for yourself. Why do you ask me? If you are willing, pay down the price, and make an end of the business." "If I buy you," said Xanthus, "you will try to escape." "If I do," said Æsop, "I shall not come to you for advice, as you do now to me." "But thou art deformed!" "A philosopher," replied Æsop, "should not only view the body, but examine the mind." The scholars, pleased with his ingenious replies, again requested Xanthus to buy him. He therefore asked the merchant what price was set upon him; who answered, "Surely thy design is to debase my commodities. Thou hast declined the best to take the worst." However, Xanthus, desirous of buying him, again asked the price; which, when known, the scholars paid, and Xanthus took him into possession.

When they came near home Xanthus commanded Æsop to wait in the porch, lest his deformity should offend his wife; whom Xanthus thus addressed:— "Mistress, you shall have no cause for the future to be discontented, for there is a servant in the porch as handsome as ever was beheld." At this the maids smiled, and contended who should first oblige him. The wife of Xanthus ordered one of them to fetch him. Æsop, overhearing her, prepared to enter. The maid, amazed at his deformity, cried, "Art thou he?" "Yes, sure," said Æsop. "Enter not," replied the maid, "unless you mean to frighted us all out of the house." But Æsop persisted, and appeared before his mistress, who, upon seeing him, thus addressed Xanthus:— "What monster is this you have brought? Discharge him instantly." At the same time declaring he had much offended her, and desiring he would return that with which she had enriched him, and she would abandon that unhappy mansion. On this Xanthus rebuked Æsop, who had discovered so much ingenuity before, that he was so silent now. "Cast her off," said Æsop. "Away with you, villain," replied he. "My love and my life is so incorporated into hers, as if one heart alone managed two bodies." At which Æsop, stamping, said that Xanthus was under the dominion of his wife; and turning to his mistress, said, "You, madam, would have had the philosopher have brought you a young, handsome fellow, whose attractions might feed your vanity, but at the same time might endanger his reputation. Oh, Euripides, thy mouth was a golden one, for these words came out of it!—'Great is the effort of the sea when its waves swell into sedition, and obey no law; and the flame or impression of devouring fire; poverty, is a ruinous condition; and there are many things intolerable, but nothing equal to an impetuous woman.' You, being the wife of a philososher, should not be attended by such persons as would bring philosophy itself into disrepute." She, being unable to contradict him, asked Xanthus where he had purchased this beauty. "The handsomeness of his ingenuity," said she, "doth recompense for the deformity of his person: my dislike of him is extinguished." "Your mistress," said Xanthus to Æsop, "is now reconciled." Æsop ironically replied, "'Tis a difficult matter sure to appease a woman." "For the future," said Xanthus, "be silent; I bought you to obey, not to contradict."

The day following, Xanthus, going to the garden to buy herbs, commanded Æsop to accompany him. When the gardener had gathered the herbs, he entrusted them to Æsop. When they were paid for, the gardener asked Xanthus what was the natural reason that the herbs that he planted did not improve with that quick and active growth, as those which were Nature's voluntary production? Xanthus, not being able to answer the question, thus replied : — "It thus happened from that order and series of Providence that threaded together inferior causes and their effects." — At which Æsop smiled. "Do you laugh at me?" said Xanthus. "I laugh at you," answered he, "and not you only, but him that taught you." Upon which Xanthus, addressing himself to the gardener, said, "It is not fit for me, who have disputed in learned auditories, to unravel questions in a garden. My servant here will solve the difficulty." The gardener replied, "Is there any knowledge treasured up in this sordid vessel?" At which Æsop was offended, and asked the gardener this question : "When a widow is engaged in second nuptials she is mother to the issue of her first marriage, but stepmother to the children of her second husband. Those, to whom by the proper obligations of Nature her affections are entitled, she affects and values more than those to whom she is mother only by accidental relation. So it is here — the earth is a stepmother to those plants which are incorporated into her womb by art, but a mother to those which are her own free production." The gardener was so well satisfied with his reply that he gave him liberty to gather what herbs he might at any time want, as a recompense.

Some days after this, Xanthus, having met with some friends at the bath, and intending to invite them to dinner, ordered Æsop to go directly home,

and boil some lentils. He went, as enjoined, and
only boiled one. Xanthus, after bathing, accordingly invited his friends, informing them, that
though their fare would be scanty, yet he was confident they would take the will for the deed.   When
they came home Xanthus ordered Æsop to bring
something to drink; who, taking some water from
the stream of the bath, presented it to Xanthus; at
which he was offended, and asked Æsop where he
brought it from?   "From the bath," said Æsop.
Xanthus, on account of his friends, concealed his
anger, and called for a basin, which Æsop having
brought, stood still. Xanthus asked him, "Do you
not wash?" He replied, "'T is for you to command,
me to obey, but to put water in the basin was no
part of the command." Upon which Xanthus asked
his friends whether they thought he had bought. a
servant: who replied, that, in their opinion, he had
rather purchased a master. Xanthus now asked if
dinner was ready? When Æsop, putting the lentil
into a shell, presented it to his master; who, having
tried if it was boiled enough, ordered him to serve
up the rest. Æsop immediately put the broth into
saucers, and brought them to Xanthus ; who asked
where the lentils were ? "You have it already,"
replied Æsop. "Did you boil but one ?" said his
master. "No more, sir," said Æsop; "Your command was in the singular number." At which Xanthus incensed, exclaimed, "This fellow is enough
to drive me mad ! but, that I may not deceive my
friends, go instantly, and buy four hogs' feet, and
boil them." Which Æsop cheerfully did. Now,
while they were boiling, Xanthus, wishing to find
some cause of complaint, in Æsop's absence took

out one of the feet ; which Æsop on his return missed, and, suspecting the design, ran to an adjacent
hog-sty, and, cutting off one of the feet of a fatted
hog, singed it, and put it into the pot. Xanthus,
suspecting that Æsop, on the discovery, would run
away, put the foot in again. So that, when Æsop
came to serve them up on the table, he found there
were five. Upon which Xanthus inquired by what
means they were multiplied. Æsop answered by
asking, "How many feet have two hogs ?"—His
master replied, "Eight." "Here, then," said Æsop,
" are five present, and yon fatted hog hath the other
three." Xanthus, being more enraged at this, exclaimed, "Did not I say this fellow would drive me
mad ?"

Shortly afterwards one of the scholars invited
Xanthus and his fellow students to a feast ; where
Xanthus, wishing to reconcile the difference he had
occasioned when he first returned, sent Æsop with a
choice dish to his mistress, telling him to give it to
her that loved him best. Æsop went ; and, seating
himself in the porch, called his mistress, and showed
her the present Xanthus had sent to her that loved
him best. "But this," said he, "madam, is not for
you." Then, calling his master's bitch, Lycæna, he
cast it down, and bid her eat it. At his return Xanthus asked him whether he had done as he was ordered ? He said, "Yes, and she swallowed it in my
presence." His master then inquired what she said.
"Nothing to me," said Æsop, "but to you she re-
turns her thanks." This so offended his mistress
that she determined to leave the house. In the
mean time, while they were all heated with wine,
one of the company asked, when would be the time

of the greatest confusion among mortals? Æsop replied, "When the dead rise and attempt to trace out their ancient possessions." At which the scholars smiled. Another asked why sheep lie so calmly, and swine with such an offensive noise? "The sheep," answered Æsop, "being used to be shorn, are silent, and expect nothing but what is customary; but swine, unaccustomed to be handled, when they are killed, make an hideous noise." The scholars were so pleased with his answers that they burst into laughter. Supper being over, Xanthus returned home, and would have saluted his wife; but she, being highly offended at what had passed, told him she would have nothing to say to him, who, instead of sending her his dainties, had sent them to his dog. Xanthus, surprised, asked Æsop to whom he had presented them; who replied, "To her that loves you best." Then, calling the spaniel, "This is she," said he, "for, though you load her with stripes, yet still she fawns upon and accompanies you. You should have told me to present them to your wife."—"You are now convinced, mistress," said Xanthus, "it was not my fault that the present miscarried. Bear the disappointment with patience, and I will take an opportunity of avenging it upon Æsop." But this did not satisfy his wife. She therefore went to her father; which caused Æsop to triumph, saying, "Now, sir you see which loves you best."

After this Æsop, observing his master uneasy on account of his wife's departure, told him not to be unhappy, for that he would soon bring her back again. For which purpose he set off to market, and purchased fowls, geese, &c. With these he intentionally went to the house where his mistress resided and asked the servants if they had anything to sell that would add to the magnificence of a wedding feast he was about to provide. They inquiring whose marriage was going to be celebrated, he replied, " Xanthus means to celebrate his second nuptials to-morrow." This intelligence soon reached the ear of his wife; and filled her so with jealousy that she flew home, and declared that no second espousals of his should be established but upon her urn. Thus Æsop, who was the occasion of her departure, was the cause of her hasty return.

Not long after Xanthus invited his scholars to dinner, and ordered Æsop to furnish the feast with the choicest dainties; who while fulfilling the command of his master, was studying how to expose his folly. He therefore laid out the money in tongues, which he served up accompanied with a poignant sauce.

The scholars much commended his first course, as it furnished them with matter for conversation; but the second and third being the same, the guests were astonished as well as their master; who inquired if there was nothing provided but tongues? Æsop replied, "Nothing else." — 'Thou lump of deformity," said Xanthus, "did I not command you to prepare the choicest dainties?" — "Sir," said Æsop, " your reproof before philosophers deserves my thanks. What excels the tongue? It is the great channel of learning and philosophy. By this noble organ addresses, commerce, contracts, eulogies, and marriages, are completely established. On this moves life itself. Therefore nothing is equal to the tongue." The scholars, departing, declared that the philosophy excelled that of Xanthus,

Some time after this Xanthus, perceiving the dissatisfaction of his scholars, told them it was not his design so to have treated them. "But now," said he, "I have ordered my servant to procure the worst meats for supper." Æsop, however, (constant to his purpose,) again provided tongues. Xanthus, more incensed still, asked him if this was the entertainment he had ordered? To which Æsop replied that he had exactly fulfilled his commands. "For what," said he, "is worse than the tongue? Is it not frequently the ruin of empires, cities, and private connections? Is it not the conveyance of calumnies and forgeries? In short, is it not the grand disturber of civil society?" When the scholars heard his reply, they declared that the deformity of his body was but the transcript of his distorted and irregular manners; and gave Xanthus a caution, lest his behavior should drive him out of his mind. To whom Æsop observed, that their speech betrayed their malice, by endeavoring to cause discontent between him and his master.

Xanthus, still desirous to revenge himself for these affronts, again sought for cause to complain of Æsop; and commanded him (since he had accused the scholars of officiousness) to find a man that regarded nothing. The next day, while traversing the streets, sop discovered Æono sitting in a negligent posture, void of reflection. This man Æsop accosted, and invited to dinner with his master. The clown, without hesitation, followed him, and sat down at his master's table in his mean attire. Xanthus immediately asked who this guest was? Æsop replied, "It is a person regardless." Xanthus then desired his wife to wash the stranger's feet, thinking he would not permit her. But, when she offered, the clown carelessly stretched out his feet for the purpose, and suffered her to perform the office. Xanthus next ordered him a goblet of wine, which he readily drank off. When the meat was set before him, Xanthus complained that it was not enough seasoned ; but the clown said he thought it was very agreeable. Whereupon Xanthus, troubled because he could not discompose him, ordered the cheesecakes to be brought, which the stranger also disposed of. Upon this, Xanthus blamed the baker for not mingling honey and pepper in the cheesecakes. The baker said it was not his fault, but that of his mistress. Xanthus then said, if it was so, that she should be instantly burnt alive, thinking the clown would attempt her rescue. But he, seeing no occasion for so prodigious a passion, desired Xanthus to wait until he brought his wife also, that they might both suffer together. Upon this Xanthus acknowledged that Æsop had punctually fulfilled his command, for which he would shortly grant him his freedom.

The next day Xanthus sent Æsop to the bath, to inform him what company was there. As he was going he met the city prætor ; who (knowing him to be the servant of Xanthus) asked him where he was going. Æsop answered, "I do not know." At which the prætor was offended, and ordered him to prison for speaking so impertinently. As they were taking him away, he cried out, "Oh, prætor, did I not tell you I did not know where I was going?" The prætor, pleased with the reply, dismissed him ; and Æsop went on his errand. Observing that many stumbled, both going in and coming out of the bath, at a stone which lay at the entrance, and that only one attempted to lay it aside, he went home, and told his master there was but one person in the bath. Xanthus arriving, and seeing a multitude, asked him the reason of his false information. Æsop told him, there was a great stone lay at the entrance, over which many stumbled, but only one removed the obstacle; so that there was only one man, the rest being little better than ciphers.

Not long after, on a day fixed by Xanthus and other philosophers for public rejoicing. Xanthus having drank freely, was raised into a passion, being worsted in some dispute that had arisen; which Æsop observing, said. "Master, Bacchus is the parent of three evils. The first is voluptuousness, the second intemperance, the third calumny or reproach; of which you, being engaged in drink, should beware." At last, Xanthus being intoxicated, one of the scholars asked him if it was possible to drink off the sea. "Very easy," said Xanthus, "I will engage to perform it myself." Upon which they laid a wager; and having exchanged rings, departed. The day following Xanthus missed his ring, and asked Æsop what was become of it. "I know not," said he, "but this I am confident of — we must not stay here; for yesterday, when disguised with liquor, you betted your whole fortune that you would drink off the ocean; and, to bind the wager, you exchanged your ring." Xanthus replied, "What could I engage less? But can you contrive how to get rid of it?" — "To perform it," said Æsop, "is impossible; but how to avoid it I will show you. When you meet again, be as confident as ever, and order a table to be placed on the shore, and persons prepared to lave the ocean with cups; and, when the multi-

tude are assembled, ask what was the wager. The
reply will be, that you engaged to drink up the sea:
then do you address them thus,—' Ye citizens of
Samos, you are not ignorant that many rivers discharge themselves into the sea. My agreement was
to drink up the ocean, and not those streams. If
you, then, can obstruct their course, I am ready to
perform my engagement. " Xanthus, being pleased
with the expedient, when the people assembled, acted and said as Æsop had instructed him ; for which
he was highly applauded. When the scholar fell at
his feet, and owned himself wrong, at the same time
requesting that the wager might be dissolved ; which
Xanthus, at the desire of the Samians, granted.

Æsop, on his return home, intimated to Xanthus
how much he had merited his freedom, that he had
bid him go to the door; and, if there were two crows
in sight, to tell him, for it was an auspicious omen ;.
but, if he beheld but one, it would be a bad one.
Æsop returned, and told him he saw two perched
on a tree. But, when Xanthus went out, one of
them was gone. Upon which he called Æsop an ungrateful villain, observing that his whole aim was
to make him an object of ridicule, for which he
should now be scourged. Æsop, groaning with his
stripes, addressed one who entered to sup with his
master, in a sad accent, thus : "You, that beheld
one crow, are rewarded with a supper ; and I, that
discovered two, am recompensed undeservedly."
Which ingenious address so softened Xanthus, that
he forbade the continuance of his punishment.

Shortly after, Xanthus designing to entertain the
philosophers and orators, commanded Æsop to stand
at the gate, and admit none but wise men. At the

appointed time several came to the gate, requesting
admittance: but Æsop put this question to them all
—"What stirs the dog?" At which they were much
offended, supposing he meant to give them that ap-
pellation.   At last one came who made this reply
to his question,   " His ears and his tail." Æsop,
satisfied with the answer, admitted him, and conducted him to his master, saying there was only one
philosopher had desired admittance. The day following, when they met at the schools, they reproached Xanthus with treating them contemptuously, by
permitting Æsop to stand at the gate and salute
them with the opprobrious epithet of "dogs." Xanthus asked if they were serious. They replied, they
were. Upon which Æsop was called, and asked
how he dared to affront his friends ? To which he
replied, " Did you not tell me that none but philosophers should be admitted ?"— "And what are
these ?" said Xanthus, "do they not merit that
character ?"   "By no means," said Æsop, " for,
when they came to the gate, I demanded of them—
What stirs the dog? and but one among them all
gave a proper answer." Upon this all agreed that
Æsop had acted strictly as his master commanded
him.

One day, when Xanthus, accompanied by Æsop,
went to visit the monuments, and to amuse himself
with the inscriptions, Æsop, seeing these letters on
one of them, sc. " a, b, d, o, e, θ, x." showed them
to Xanthus, asking him their meaning. Who, after
serious consideration, confessed he knew not. "Master," said Æsop, " if by these characters I trace out
a treasure, what reward shall I receive?" Xanthus
answered, " Thy freedom, and half the treasure,"

Then Æsop, having dug the earth four feet from the stone, found it; and, giving it to his master, claimed his reward. "No," said Xanthus, "not till I can unravel the mystery, the knowledge of which will be worth more than the treasure." Æsop told him a prudent man had engraven them, and the sense was this "*a* going, *b* paces, *d* four, *o* digging, *e* thou shalt find, *0* a treasure, *x* of gold!" Xanthus answered, "It will be more to my interest to keep thee than to let thee go." "Then," said Æsop, "I will prove that the gold belongs to the king of Bizantium." How do you prove it?" said his master. "Thus." replied he, "*a* restore, *b* to the king, *d* Dionysius, *o* which, *e* thou hast found, *0* treasure, *x* of gold." Upon this Xanthus requested Æsop to accept the half, as a reward for his silence. Æsop replied, "I receive not this as the effect of your bounty, but of his who concealed it; for this is the genuine sense of the letters—*a* taking, *b* go your way, *d* divide, *o* which, *e* you have found, *0* the treasure." Xanthus replied, "Come, depart; the moiety of the gold, and your freedom, shall be your reward." As they returned, Xanthus (fearing Æsop would discover the affair) commanded that they should take him to prison. As they were taking him away, Æsop exclaimed, "Do the solemn promises of philosophers, and their specious intimation of liberty end in prison and fetters?" Upon which Xanthus ordered his release, observing that what he had said was true; though he was confident, when he had got his freedom, he would do all that lay in his power to injure him. Æsop answered, "In spite of all your artifices, I shall obtain my liberty."

Soon after this, on a day appointed for general festivity by the citzens of Samos, an eagle descended, snatched up the public ring, and afterwards dropped it into the lap of a slave. The astonished Samians applied to Xanthus to unfold the mystery ; who, knowing himself incapable, was very much dejected. Æsop, perceiving this, asked what made him so unhappy. "To-morrow, when you appear in public," says he, "tell the Samians, that you are not dexterous in these matters, but you have a servant that is." To this Xanthus agreed, and accordingly the next day Æsop was called forth. But, when they saw him, they smiled, asking contemptuously, "How can such a deformed creature unfold this great mystery?" Æsop, waving his hand, replied, "Ye citizens of Samos, you should not only view the front of the house, but the tenant also; for frequently an upright and understanding soul dwells in a deformed and disordered body; and you know it is not the shape of the cask that men admire, but the wine concealed therein." Hearing this, they desired him to proceed: wherefore he continued, "Ye Samians, it rests with you to judge between the master and the servant. If I do not unfold the mystery concealed in this signal accident, let stripes be my reward; but, if the master be outvied by the discovery, then let my freedom be given me." Upon this they insisted that Xanthus should give Æsop his freedom. Xanthus making no reply, the city prætor addressed him thus:—"If you do not grant the request of the people, I will declare Æsop free." Whereupon Xanthus declared Æsop free and the city crier proclaimed it. Then said Æsop to his master, "In spite of your malice, I have obtained my freedom." And then, addressing the people, he thus unfolded the mystery: " Ye citizens of Samos ! the eagle, you know, is the monarch of birds ; and, as the public ring was dropped into the lap of a slave, it seems to forebode that some of the adjacent kings will attempt to overthrow your established laws, and entomb your liberty in slavery."

This filled the Samians with grief. Shortly after, letters arrived from Crœsus of Lydia, requiring the Samians to pay tribute, or else prepare to suffer the calamities of a destructive war.

Upon which a public council was called, and Æsop was requested to give his advice; who thus addressed them . "We have," said have, "but two objects before us. The one is liberty; which in the beginning is rough and difficult, but in the end is smooth and easy; and the other is bondage ; whose beginning is easy, but the conclusion fatal and calamitous." The Samians, when they heard this, declard, that, as they were at present free, so they and their liberty would stand or fall together ;—and with this resolute reply dismissed the ambassadors. Crœsus being informed of their resolution, determined to go to war with them. But the ambassadors advised him first to send for Æsop, with the promise that the tribute should be suspended, and then perhaps he might reduce them; but that, as long as they were strengthened with the counsels of Æsop, he would not be able. Crœsus took their advice, and sent for him on those conditions. The Samians, being well satisfied, agreed to give him up. But, when Æsop heard of it, he thus addressed them : " Ye citizens of Samos, I am ready to prostrate myself at the feet of Crœsus, but first I will tell you a tale. The wolves commenced war with the sheep, but the sheep were secured by the generous protection of the dogs; on which the wolves sent ambassadors to the sheep, to this end, that, if they desired peace, they should give up their dogs. The timorous and unwary sheep agreed to it, and sent away their protectors. The wolves immediately destroyed their dogs, and then the sheep fell an easy prey." The Samians, comprehending his meaning, refused to let Æsop go, but he re·solved to accompany the ambassadors.

When they arrived at Lydia, they presented Æsop. As soon as the king saw him he was angry; despising the idea that so despicable a person should by his counsels prevent him from conquering the Samians. Æsop, observing his astonishment, said, "Mighty sir! since neither by force nor necessity, but of my own free will, I give myself up, I request your attention. A certain man, having gathered many locusts, killed them; and having with them taken a grasshopper, she thus bespoke him: 'Sir, do not kill me, for I am no ways destructive, my whole employment being to charm to sleep the weary traveller.' Upon which he let her go. Thus I, O king, prostrate before you, desire my life may be the monument of your mercy, since it cannot be prejudicial to any man; for in this deformed body you shall find an exalted mind." Crœsus replied, "Æsop, not only thy life, but a fortune, shall be the proof of my beneficence. Demand, therefore, what you please, and it shall be granted." "Oh king," said Æsop, "be reconciled to the Samians." The king replied, "I am." And shortly after sent Æsop back with letters of reconciliation. On his arrival, the citizens, crowned with garlands, saluted him, rejoicing to find that peace was re-established.

He not long after departed from Samos; and, after passing through many kingdoms, and disputing with several philosophers, at last arrived at Babylon; where he soon gained the esteem of King Lycerus. In those days it was usual for nations to send philosophical questions to each other, subject to a fine if they could not resolve them. Now Æsop, unfolding those sent to King Lycerus, improved the reputation of the king. He also, in the king's name, proposed many; which the neighboring kings were not able to resolve.

Æsop, being childless, had adopted a nobleman named Eunus for his heir, and sought the favor of the king in his behalf. But one day, surprising him with his concubine, he discarded him. In revenge for which, Eunus forged letters from Æsop to the philosophers of another kingdom, and presented them to King Lycerus; in which it appeared that Æsop wished to render them services in preference to the king.

The king, believing the imposture, without examining into the truth of it, ordered Hermippus to put Æsop to death. But he, being in friendship with Æsop, concealed him in a sepulchre. The king gave Æsop's estates to Eunus.

Not long after this, Nectenabo, king of Egypt, hearing Æsop was dead, sent a letter to Lycerus, requiring artificers who could erect a tower which should neither touch heaven nor earth, and one that could resolve all that was demanded; on the accomplishmnnt of which he would pay him tribute; but, in case of failure, he would exact it of him. After the king had read the letter he cried out, " Æsop, the pillar of my kingdom, is dead ! " Now Hermippus, hearing the king deplore his loss, informed him he had not performed his command, but had preserved the life of Æsop ; well knowing that the king himself would in the end be grieved.

At which the king rejoiced, and sent for Æsop ; who, after having established his innocence, was again received into favor, and Eunus was condemned to die ; but, on the intercession of Æsop, his life was spared. Now, as soon as the King of Egypt's letter was shown to Æsop, he desired that this message might be returned — " that, after winter was expired, one should appear who would not only erect the tower, but answer every question demanded." Which was immediately dispatched. Æsop, having readopted Eunus, admonished him to this effect : " My son, worship God, and honor the king; make thyself a terror to thine enemies, and useful to thy friends. Pray that thine enemies may be indigent, that they may not offend thee; and thy friends opulent, that they may be able to assist thee. Be constant to thy consort, lest thy inconstancy should make her so. Be slow to speak and swift to hear. Envy not those who do well. So manage thy domestic affairs that those who fear may love. Be not ashamed to learn. Trust not thy secrets to a woman, lest she should be insolent. Let to-day's stock be the pledge of to-morrow's store. Be gentle to all. Discard parasites and whisperers. Always act as thou mayest have no cause to repent." These sayings had such an effect upon Eunus, that he shortly after died with remorse and compunction.

The winter being nearly expired, Æsop procured four young eagles; which he taught to carry baskets with little children in them, and to obey their command; and, having prepared for his journey into Egypt, in a short time set off, taking the eagles with him.

Nectenabo, being told that Æsop was arrived, expressed his surprise, having understood that he was dead. The next day all his officers were assembled, dressed in white robes; and the king in his royal attire and imperial diadem. When seated on his throne he sent for Æsop, and asked him, to what he resembled him, and those who surrounded the throne? Æsop replied, "You resemble the vernal sun, and your attendants a fruitful harvest." With which answer the king was greatly pleased. The day following the king appeared in white, and his retinue in purple; when Æsop was asked the same question: to which he answered, "You are an emblem of the sun, and those that stand round a type of effused beams." Then Nectenabo inquired his opinion of his kingdom, and whether he did not think it preferable to that of Lycerus. "Do not flatter yourself," said Æsop, "though your kingdom may shine like the rays of the sun, yet, if put into competition with his, it would soon fade." Nectenabo, applauding his answer, asked where they were that could erect the tower. "They are ready," said Æsop, "if you have appointed the place." Upon which the king showed him a spacious plain. Then Æsop produced the eagles, with the children in the baskets; and, giving them their working instruments, commanded the eagles to fly, who, being raised in the air, demanded the necessary materials.

Nectenabo, hearing their request, said to Æsop, "I have no men that can fly." Æsop replied, "How then can you think of engaging in a contest with King Lycerus, who is stored with such?" Nectenabo acknowledged himself subdued.

Shortly after he sent for several sages from Heliopolis, to ask Æsop a variety of questions. One of the Heliopolitans at the banquet said to Æsop, "I am employed by one of our deities to ask you this question."—"You discover your ignorance," said Æsop, "by diminishing the knowledge of one of your gods." A second put this question, desiring Æsop to explain it: "There is a vast temple, and a column supporting twelve magnificent cities, each of which is sustained with thirty rafters, and constantly circulated by two women." To this Æsop answered, "The temple is the world, the cities the months, the rafters the days of the month, and the day and night are the two women who successively attend each other."

The day following Nectenabo summoned his friends, and confessed that the tribute exacted by Lycerus was due to the ingenuity of Æsop. One of them replied, "We will try him again with questions that were never heard of." "And I," said Æsop, "will answer them."

He then departed, and prepared a schedule, whereon was engrossed — "Nectenabo confesses he is indebted a thousand talents to Lycerus." And in the morning presented it to the king; who, paying him the money, observed that Lycerus was fortunate to have his kingdom supported by so sagacious a person. He then dismissed him, bidding him farewell.

Æsop, having digested the whole into a narrative, returned to Babylon, and presented it with the tribute to Lycerus; who was so well pleased, that he commanded an elegant statue to be erected to his memory.

Shortly after he obtained leave of the king to sail into Greece, upon condition that he should return to Babylon. Having surveyed the different provinces, and obtained an eminent character, he set off for Delphos, where the temple of Apollo stood. But here they paid but little attention to his eloquence ; observing which, Æsop said, "Ye citizens of Delphos you justly resemble the wood that floats on the sea ; which at a distance appears something worth, but when it approaches we are disappointed. So I, when at a great distance from your city, did admire you, but now am led to think you the most useless among men." Hearing this, they were afraid that he would, at his departure, speak disrespectfully of them; they therefore determined to ensnare and destroy him. For which end they took a golden cup out of the temple, and concealed it in Æsop's baggage ; who, unsuspecting, departed to Phocide. The Delphians pursued him, and there charged him with sacrilege. He denied the fact, but they untied his baggage, found the cup, and discovered it to the city. Æsop, now seeing through their malicious stratagem, desired they would not deprive him of his life. But they first condemned him to prison, and then to death. Æsop, unable to extricate himself, deplored his fate in the prison. While he was complaining, one Demas (a friend) asked him the cause of his violent sorrow. Æsop replied, "A woman, having lately buried her husband, wept daily over his grave. One, who was plowing not far off, fell in love with her; and, leaving his oxen, went to the grave, and mourned with her. She asked why he wept. 'Because,' replied he, 'I have lately buried an amiable wife, and find it gives me ease.'—'Such is my fate,' said the woman. 'Then,' said he, 'as we are united in trouble, why should we not be joined in marriage, since we love each other?' While they were thus engaged some villain took away his oxen; upon which he went home and wept much. The woman inquired, why he wept now. He replied, 'I have just cause to weep.' So I, after having escaped many dangers, have cause to weep that I cannot extricate myself from this. The Delphians then came, and dragged him to the verge of a craggy precipice; when Æsop thus addressed them: "When beasts did parley, the mouse, being intimate with the frog, invited her to supper in the storehouse of a rich man, desiring her to make herself welcome. After this the frog invited the mouse; and, that he might not be tired of swimming, she tied his leg to hers. This done, they endeavored to go across the stream; but, before they were half over, the mouse was drowned; and, when dying, declared the frog was the cause, and that some more powerful than themselves would avenge his death. The eagle, beholding the mouse floating on the water, snatched at him, and with him took the frog; thus both fell a prey to the eagle. So I, who am ready to fall a victim to your injustice, shall not want an avenger; for all Greece and Babylon will unite for that purpose."

But all this was of no avail; neither his attempt to shelter himself in the temple. They still continued dragging him to the precipice ; when he again addressed them : " Ye citizens of Delphos, the hare, being pursued by the eagle, retreated into the nest of the hornet. The hornet implored the eagle to have pity on the hare. The eagle repulsed the hornet, and destroyed the hare. The hornet traced out the nest of the eagle, and demolished her eggs. The next time the eagle built her nest higher; but the hornet still pursued, and again destroyed them. The third time the eagle soared, and deposited her eggs between the knees of Jupiter, invoking his protection. The hornet, composing a ball of dirt, dropped it into Jupiter's lap ; who, forgetting the egg, shook all off together. Being informed by the hornet that this was in revenge for a former injury, he endeavored to reconcile them, lest the progeny of his favorite bird should be destroyed. But, the· hornet persisting, he respited the hatching of the eagles till the time when the hornets sally forth. And you, citizens of Delphos, despise not this deity, from whom I have implored refuge."

Now Æsop, perceiving they continued still deaf to his entreaties, sternly, and for the last time, bespoke them thus : " Ye cruel and obdurate men, a certain husbandman, growing aged, who had never beheld the city, desired his servants to convey him thither, that he might see it before he died. As he went he was overtaken by a violent storm and gloomy darkness, so that the asses which drew the carriage mistook the way, and guided him to a precipice ; where, being upon the verge of approaching ruin, he thus exclaimed : ' Oh Jove, what injury have I committed, that hath incensed thee to cause this misfortune; especially that I should owe my death not to generous horses, nor to active mules, but to dull and despicable asses?" "And this," said Æsop, "is my unhappy fate, not by the hands of persons of worth and abilities, but by those of the vilest and most worthless of men." This said, the Delphians threw him from the precipice, and he perished.

Not long after, a destructive pestilence having raged among them, they were told by the oracle, that it was the expiation of Æsop's unjust tragedy. Wherefore, in order to avert the judgment, they erected a pompous monument over his bones.

But, when the principals of Greece and the Sages were informed of the catastrophe, and having maturely weighed the fact, they severely revenged the innocent effusion of Æsop's blood.

LIST OF ILLUSTRATIONS.

FABLES OF ÆSOP.

THE LION AND THE MOUSE.

A LION was awakened from sleep by a Mouse running over his face. Rising up in anger, he caught him and was about to kill him, when the Mouse piteously entreated, saying: "If you would only spare my life, I would be sure to repay your kindness." The Lion laughed and let him go. It happened shortly after this that the Lion was caught by some hunters, who bound him by strong ropes to the ground. The Mouse, recognizing his roar, came up, and gnawed the rope with his teeth, and setting him free, exclaimed: "You ridiculed the idea of my ever being able to help you, not expecting to receive from me any repayment of your favor; but now you know that it is possible for even a Mouse to confer benefits on a Lion."

THE FATHER AND HIS SONS.

A FATHER had a family of sons who were perpetually quarrelling among themselves. When he failed to heal their disputes by his exhortations, he determined to give them a practical illustration of the evils of disunion; and for this purpose he one day told them to bring him a bundle of sticks. When they had done so, he placed the faggot into the hands of each of them in succession, and ordered them to break it in pieces. They each tried with all their strength, and were not able to do it. He next unclosed the faggot, and took the sticks separately, one by one, and again put them into their hands, on which they broke them easily. He then addressed them in these words: "My sons, if you are of one mind, and unite to assist each other, you will be as this faggot, uninjured by all the attempts of your enemies; but if you are divided among yourselves, you will be broken as easily as these sticks."

THE WOLF AND THE LAMB.

A Wolf meeting with a Lamb astray from the fold, resolved not to lay violent hands on him, but to find some plea, which should justify to the Lamb himself his right to eat him. He thus addressed him: "Sirrah, last year you grossly insulted me." "Indeed," bleated the Lamb in a mournful tone of voice, "I was not then born." Then said the Wolf, "You feed in my pasture." "No, good sir," replied the Lamb, "I have not yet tasted grass." Again said the Wolf, "You drink of my well." "No," exclaimed the Lamb, "I never yet drank water, for as yet my mother's milk is both food and drink to me." On which the Wolf seized him, and ate him up, saying, "Well! I won't remain supperless, even though you refute every one of my imputations."

The tyrant will always find a pretext for his tyranny.

THE BAT AND THE WEASELS.

A BAT falling upon the ground was caught by a Weasel, of whom he earnestly sought his life. The Weasel refused, saying, that he was by nature the enemy of all birds. The Bat assured him that he was not a bird, but a mouse, and thus saved his life. Shortly afterwards the Bat again fell on the ground, and was caught by another Weasel, whom he likewise entreated not to eat him. The Weasel said that he had a special hostility to mice. The Bat assured him that he was not a mouse, but a bat; and thus a second time escaped.

It is wise to turn circumstances to good account.

THE ASS AND THE GRASSHOPPER.

AN Ass having heard some Grasshoppers chirping, was highly enchanted; and, desiring to possess the same charms of melody, demanded what sort of food they lived on, to give them such beautiful voices. They replied, "The dew." The Ass resolved that he would only live upon dew, and in a short time died of hunger.

THE WOLF AND THE CRANE.

A WOLF, having a bone stuck in his throat, hired a Crane, for a large sum, to put her head into his throat and draw out the bone. When the Crane had-extracted the bone, and demanded the promised payment, the Wolf, grinning and grinding his teeth, exclaimed: "Why, you have surely already a sufficient recompense, in having been permitted to draw out your head in safety from the mouth and jaws of a Wolf."

In serving the wicked, expect no reward, and be thankful if you escape injury for your pains.

THE CHARCOAL-BURNER AND THE FULLER.

A Charcoal-burner carried on his trade in his own house. One day he met a friend, a Fuller, and entreated him to come and live with him, saying, that they should be far better neighbors, and that their housekeeping expenses would be lessened. The Fuller replied: "The arrangement is impossible as far as I am concerned, for whatever I should whiten, you would immediately blacken again with your charcoal."

Like will draw like.

THE BOY HUNTING LOCUSTS.

A Boy was hunting for locusts. He had caught a goodly number, when he saw a Scorpion, and, mistaking him for a locust, reached out his hand to take him. The Scorpion, showing his sting, said: "If you had but touched me, my friend, you would have lost me, and all your locusts too!"

THE ANTS AND THE GRASSHOPPER.

The Ants were employing a fine winter's day in drying grain collected in the summer time. A Grasshopper, perishing with famine, passed by and earnestly begged for a little food. The Ants inquired of him, "Why did you not treasure up food during the summer?" He replied, "I had not leisure enough. I passed the days in singing." They then said in derision: "If you were foolish enough to sing all the summer, you must dance supperless to bed in the winter."

THE COCK AND THE JEWEL.

A Cock, scratching for food for himself and his hens, found a precious stone; on which he said: "If your owner had found thee, and not I, he would have taken thee up, and have set thee in thy first estate; but I have found thee for no purpose. I would rather have one barleycorn than all the jewels in the world."

THE KINGDOM OF THE LION.

THE beasts of the field and forest had a Lion as their king. He was neither wrathful, cruel, nor tyrannical, but just and gentle as a king could be. He made during his reign a royal proclamation for a general assembly of all the birds and beasts, and drew up conditions for an universal league, in which the Wolf and the Lamb, the Panther and the Kid, the Tiger and the Stag, the Dog and the Hare, should live together in perfect peace and amity. The Hare said, "Oh, how I have longed to see this day, in which the weak shall take their place with impunity by the side of the strong."

THE FISHERMAN PIPING.

A FISHERMAN skilled in music took his flute and his nets to the sea-shore. Standing on a projecting rock he played several tunes, in the hope that the fish, attracted by his melody, would of their own accord dance into his net, which he had placed below. At last, having long waited in vain, he laid aside his flute, and casting his net into the sea, made an excellent haul of fish. When he saw them leaping about in the net upon the rock he said: "O you most perverse creatures, when I piped you would not dance, but now that I have ceased you do so merrily."

THE HARE AND THE TORTOISE.

A HARE one day ridiculed the short feet and slow pace of the Tortoise. The latter, laughing, said: "Though you be swift as the wind, I will beat you in a race." The Hare, deeming her assertion to be simply impossible, assented to the proposal; and they agreed that the Fox should choose the course, and fix the goal. On the day appointed for the race they started together. The Tortoise never for a moment stopped, but went on with a slow but steady pace straight to the end of the course. The Hare, trusting to his native swiftness, cared little about the race, and laying down by the wayside, fell fast asleep. At last waking up, and moving as fast as he could, he saw the Tortoise had reached the goal, and was comfortably dozing after her fatigue.

THE TRAVELER AND HIS DOG.

A TRAVELER, about to set out on his journey, saw his Dog standing at the door stretching himself. He asked him sharply: "What do you stand gaping there for? Everything is ready but you; so come with me instantly." The Dog, wagging his tail, replied: "O, master! I am quite ready; it is you for whom I am waiting."

The loiterer often imputes delay to his more active friend.

HERCULES AND THE WAGONER.

A CARTER was driving a wagon along a country lane, when the wheels sank down deep into a rut. The rustic driver, stupified and aghast, stood looking at the wagon, and did nothing but utter loud cries to Hercules to come and help him. Hercules, it is said, appeared, and thus addressed him: "Put your shoulders to the wheels, my man. Goad on your bullocks, and never more pray to me for help, until you have done your best to help yourself, or depend upon it you will henceforth pray in vain."

Self-help is the best help.

THE DOG AND THE SHADOW.

A Dog, crossing a bridge over a stream with a piece of flesh in his mouth, saw his own shadow in the water, and took it for that of another Dog, with a piece of meat double his own in size. He therefore let go his own, and fiercely attacked the other Dog, to get his larger piece from him. He thus lost both: that which he grasped at in the water, because it was a shadow; and his own, because the stream swept it away.

THE MOLE AND HIS MOTHER.

A MOLE, a creature blind from its birth, once said to his mother: "I am sure that I can see, mother!" In the desire to prove to him his mistake, his mother placed before him a few grains of frankincense, and asked, "What is it?" The young Mole said, "It is a pebble." His mother exclaimed: "My son, I am afraid that you are not only blind, but that you have lost your sense of smell."

THE SWALLOW AND THE CROW.

THE Swallow and the Crow had a contention about their plumage. The Crow put an end to the dispute by saying: "Your feathers are all very well in the spring, but mine protect me against the winter."

Fine weather friends are not worth much.

THE FARMER AND THE SNAKE.

A FARMER found in the winter time a Snake stiff and frozen with cold. He had compassion on it, and taking it up placed it in his bosom. The Snake on being thawed by the warmth quickly revived, when, resuming its natural instincts, he bit his benefactor, inflicting on him a mortal wound. The Farmer said with his latest breath, "I am rightly served for pitying a scoundrel!"

The greatest benefits will not bind the ungrateful.

THE HERDSMAN AND THE LOST BULL.

A Herdsman tending kine in a forest, lost
a Bull-calf from the fold. After a long
and fruitless search, he made a vow that,
if he could only discover the thief

who had stolen the Calf, he would offer a lamb in sacrifice to Hermes, Pan, and the Guardian Deities of the forest. Not long afterwards, as he ascended a small hillock, he saw at its foot a Lion feeding on the Calf. Terrified at the sight, he lifted his eyes and his hands to heaven, and said: "Just now I vowed to offer a lamb to the Guardian Deities of the forest if I could only find out who had robbed me; but now that I have discovered the thief, I would willingly add a full-grown Bull to the Calf I have lost, if I may only secure my own escape from him in safety."

THE FARMER AND THE STORK.

A FARMER placed nets on his newly sown plough lands, and caught a quantity of Cranes, which came to pick up his seed. With them he trapped a Stork also. The Stork having his leg fractured by the net, earnestly besought the Farmer to spare his life. "Pray, save me, Master," he said, "and let me go free this once. My broken limb should excite your pity. Besides, I am no Crane, I am a Stork, a bird of excellent character; and see how I love and slave for my father and mother. Look too, at my feathers, they are not the least like to those of a Crane." The Farmer laughed aloud, and said, "It may be all as you say; I only know this, I have taken you with these robbers, the Cranes, and you must die in their company."

Birds of a feather flock together,

THE FAWN AND HIS MOTHER.

A Young Fawn once said to his mother, "You are larger than a dog, and swifter, and more used to running, and you have too your horns as a defence; why, then, O Mother! are you always in such a terrible fright of the hounds?" She smiled, and said: "I know full well, my son, that all you say is true. I have the advantages you mention, but yet when I hear only the bark of a single dog I feel ready to faint, and fly away as fast as I can."

No arguments will give courage to the coward,

THE POMEGRANATE, APPLE TREE, AND BRAMBLE.

The Pomegranate and Apple-tree disputed as to which was the most beautiful. When their strife was at its height, a Bramble from the neighboring hedge lifted up its voice, and said in a boastful tone: "Pray, my dear friends, in my presence at least cease from such vain disputings."

THE MOUNTAIN IN LABOR.

A Mountain was once greatly agitated. Loud groans and noises were heard; and crowds of people came from all parts to see what was the matter. While they were assembled in anxious expectation of some terrible calamity, out came a Mouse.

Don't make much ado about nothing.

THE BEAR AND THE FOX.

A Bear boasted very much of his philanthropy, saying "that of all animals he was the most tender in his regard for man, for he had such respect for him, that he would not even touch his dead body." A Fox hearing these words said with a smile to the Bear, "Oh! that you would eat the dead and not the living."

THE ASS, THE FOX, AND THE LION.

THE Ass and the Fox having entered into partnership together for their mutual protection, went out into the forest to hunt. They had not proceeded far, when they met a Lion. The Fox, seeing the imminency of the danger, approached the Lion, and promised to contrive for him the capture of the Ass, if he would pledge his word that his own life should not be endangered. On his assuring him that he would not injure him, the Fox led the Ass to a deep pit, and contrived that he should fall into it. The Lion seeing that the Ass was secured, immediately clutched the Fox, and then attacked the Ass at his leisure.

THE FLIES AND THE HONEY-POT.

A Jar of Honey having been upset in a house-keeper's room, a number of flies were attracted by its sweetness, and placing their feet in it, ate it greedily. Their feet however became so smeared with the honey that they could not use their wings, nor release themselves, and were suffocated. Just as they were expiring, they exclaimed, "O foolish creatures that we are, for the sake of a little pleasure we have destroyed ourselves."

Pleasure bought with pains, hurts.

THE MAN AND THE LION.

A Man and a Lion travelled together through the forest. They soon began to boast of their respective superiority to each other in strength and prowess. As they were disputing, they passed a statue, carved in stone, which represented "a Lion strangled by a Man." The traveller pointed to it and said: "See there! How strong we are, and how we prevail over even the king of beasts." The Lion replied: "This statue was made by one of you men. If we Lions knew how to erect statues, you would see the Man placed under the paw of the Lion."

One story is good, till another is told.

THE TORTOISE AND THE EAGLE.

A Tortoise, lazily basking in the sun, complained to the sea-birds of her hard fate, that no one would teach her to fly. An Eagle hovering near, heard her lamentation, and demanded what reward she would give him, if he would take her aloft, and float her in the air. "I will give you," she said, "all the riches of the Red Sea." "I will teach you to fly then," said the Eagle; and taking her up in his talons, he carried her almost to the clouds,—when suddenly letting her go, she fell on a lofty mountain, and dashed her shell to pieces. The Tortoise exclaimed in the moment of death: "I have deserved my present fate; for what had I to do with wings and clouds, who can with difficulty move about on the earth?"

If men had all they wished, they would be often ruined.

THE FARMER AND THE CRANES.

Some Cranes made their feeding grounds on some plough-lands newly sown with wheat. For a long time the Farmer, brandishing an empty sling, chased them away by the terror he inspired; but when the birds found that the sling was only swung in the air, they ceased to take any notice of it, and would not move. The farmer on seeing this, charged his sling with stones, and killed a great number. They at once forsook his plough-lands, and cried to each other, "It is time for us to be off to Liliput: for this man is no longer content to scare us, but begins to show us in earnest what he can do."

If words suffice not, blows must follow.

THE FOX AND THE GOAT.

A Fox having fallen into a deep well, was detained a prisoner there, as he could find no means of escape. A Goat, overcome with thirst, came to the same well, and, seeing the Fox, enquired if the water was good. The Fox, concealing his sad plight under a merry guise, indulged in a lavish praise of the water, saying it was beyond measure excellent, and encouraged him to descend. The Goat, mindful only of his thirst, thoughtlessly jumped down, when just as he quenched his thirst, the Fox informed him of the difficulty they were both in, and suggested a scheme for their common escape. "If," said he, "you will place your fore-feet upon the wall, and bend your head, I will run up your back and escape, and will help you out afterwards." On the Goat readily assenting to this second proposal, the Fox leapt upon his back, and steadying himself with the Goat's horns, reached in safety the mouth of the well, when he immediately made off as fast as he could. The Goat upbraided him with the breach of his bargain, when he turned round and cried out: "You foolish old fellow! If you had as many brains in your head as you have hairs in your beard, you would never have gone down before you had inspected the way up, nor have exposed yourself to dangers from which you had no means of escape."

Look before you leap

THE LIONESS.

A CONTROVERSY prevailed among the beasts of the field, as to which of the animals deserved the most credit for producing the greatest number of whelps at a birth. They rushed clamorously into the presence of the Lioness, and demanded of her the settlement of the dispute. "And you," they said, "how many sons have you at a birth?" The Lioness laughed at them, and said: "Why! I have only one; but that one is altogether a thorough-bred Lion."

The value is in the worth, not in the number.

THE BEAR

AND

THE TWO TRAVELERS.

Two men were traveling together, when a bear suddenly met them on their path. One of them climbed up quickly into a tree, and concealed himself in the branches. The other, seeing that he must be attacked, fell flat on the ground, and when the Bear came up and felt him with his snout, and smelt him all over, he held his breath, and feigned the appearance of death as much as he could. The Bear soon left him, for it is said he will not touch a dead body. When he was quite gone, the other traveler descended from the tree, and accosting his friend, jocularly inquired "what it was the Bear had wispered in his ear?" he replied, "He gave me this advice: Never travel with a friend who deserts you at the approach of danger."

Misfortune tests the sincerity of friends.

THE THIRSTY PIGEON.

A Pigeon, oppressed by excessive thirst, saw a goblet of water painted on a sign-board. Not supposing it to be only a picture, she flew towards it with a loud whirr, and unwittingly dashed against the sign-board and jarred herself terribly. Having broken her wings by the blow, she fell to the ground, and was caught by one of the bystanders.

Zeal should not outrun discretion.

THE OXEN AND THE AXLE-TREES.

A heavy wagon was being dragged along a country lane by a team of oxen. The axle-trees groaned and creaked terribly: when the oxen turning round, thus addressed the wheels. "Hullo there! why do you make so much noise? We bear all the labor, and we, not you, ought to cry out."

Those who suffer most cry out the least.

THE DOG IN THE MANGER.

A Dog lay in a manger, and by his growling and snapping prevented the oxen from eating the hay which had been placed for them. "What a selfish Dog!" said one of them to his companions; "he cannot eat the hay himself, and yet refuses to allow those to eat who can."

THE SICK LION.

A Lion being unable from old age and infirmities to provide himself with food by force, resolved to do so by artifice. He betook himself to his den, and lying down there, pretended to be sick, taking care that his sickness should be publicly known. The beasts expressed their sorrow, and came one by one to his den to visit him, when the Lion devoured them. After many of the beasts had thus disappeared, the Fox discovered the trick, and presenting himself to the Lion, stood on the outside of the cave, at a respectful distance, and asked of him how he did; to whom he replied, "I am very middling, but why do you stand without? pray enter within to talk with me." The Fox replied, "No, thank you, I notice that there are many prints of feet entering your cave, but I see no trace of any returning."

He is wise who is warned by the misfortunes of others.

THE RAVEN AND THE SWAN.

A Raven saw a Swan, and desired to secure for himself a like beauty of plumage. Supposing that his splendid white color arose from his washing in the water in which he swam, the Raven left the altars in the neighborhood of which he picked up his living, and took up his abode in the lakes and pools. But cleansing his feathers as often as he would, he could not change their color, while through want of food he perished.

Change of habit cannot alter nature.

THE CAT AND THE COCK.

A CAT caught a Cock, and took counsel with himself how he might find a reasonable excuse for eating him. He accused him as being a nuisance to men, by crowing in the night time, and not permitting them to sleep. The Cock defended himself by saying, that he did this for the benefit of men, that they might rise betimes for their labors. The Cat replied, "Although you abound in specious apologies, I shall not remain supperless;" and he made a meal of him.

THE BOASTING TRAVELER.

A MAN who had traveled in foreign lands, boasted very much, on returning to his own country, of the many wonderful and heroic things he had done in the different places he had visited. Among other things, he said that when he was at Rhodes he had leapt to such a distance that no man of his day could leap anywhere near him—and as to that there were in Rhodes many persons who saw him do it, and whom he could call as witnesses. One of the by-standers interrupting him, said: "Now, my good man, if this be all true there is no need of witnesses. Suppose this to be Rhodes; and now for your leap."

THE WOLF IN SHEEP'S CLOTHING.

ONCE upon a time a Wolf resolved to disguise his nature by his habit, that so he might get food without stint. Encased in the skin of a sheep, he pastured with the flock, beguiling the shepherd by his artifice. In the evening he was shut up by the shepherd in the fold; the gate was closed, and the entrance made thoroughly secure. The shepherd coming into the fold during the night to provide food for the morrow, caught up the Wolf, instead of a sheep, and killed him with his knife in the fold.

Harm seek, harm find.

THE LION IN LOVE.

A Lion demanded the daughter of a woodcutter in marriage. The Father, unwilling to grant, and yet afraid to refuse his request, hit upon this expedient to rid himself of his importunities. He expressed his willingness to accept him as the suitor of his daughter on one condition; that he should allow him to extract his teeth, and cut off his claws, as his daughter was fearfully afraid of both. The Lion cheerfully assented to the proposal: when however he next repeated his request, the woodman, no longer afraid, set upon him with his club, and drove him away into the forest.

THE GOAT AND THE GOATHERD.

A Goatherd had sought to bring back a stray goat to his flock. He whistled and sounded his horn in vain; the straggler paid no attention to the summons. At last the Goatherd threw a stone, and breaking its horn, besought the Goat not to tell his master. The Goat replied, "Why, you silly fellow, the horn will speak though I be silent."

Do not attempt to hide things which cannot be hid.

THE MISER.

A Miser sold all that he had, and bought a lump of gold, which he took and buried in a hole dug in the ground by the side of an old wall, and went daily to look at it. One of his workmen, observing his frecovered the secret of the hidden treasure, and disquent visits to the spot, watched his movements, digging down, came to the lump of gold, and stole it. The Miser, on his next visit, found the hole empty, and began to tear his hair, and to make loud lamentations. A neighbor, seeing him overcome with grief, and learning the cause, said, "Pray do not grieve so; but go and take a stone, and place it in the hole, and fancy that the gold is still lying there. It will do you quite the same service; for when the gold was there, you had it not, as you did not make the slightest use of it."

THE FROGS ASKING FOR A KING.

THE Frogs, grieved at having no established Ruler, sent ambassadors to Jupiter entreating for a King. He, perceiving their simplicity, cast down a huge log into the lake. The Frogs, terrified at the splash occasioned by its fall, hid themselves in the depths of the pool. But no sooner did they see that the huge log continued motionless, than they swam again to the top of the water, dismissed their fears, and came so to despise it as to climb up, and to squat upon it. After some time they began to think themselves ill-treated in the appointment of so inert a Ruler, and sent a second deputation to Jupiter to pray that he would set over them another sovereign. He then gave them an Eel to govern them. When the Frogs discovered his easy good nature, they yet a third time sent to Jupiter to beg that he would once more choose for them another King. Jupiter, displeased at their complaints, sent a Heron, who preyed upon the Frogs day by day, till there were none left to croak upon the Lake.

THE PORKER, THE SHEEP, AND THE GOAT.

A Young Pig was shut up in a fold-yard with a Goat and a Sheep. On one occasion the Shepherd laid hold of him, when he grunted, and squeaked, and resisted violently. The Sheep and the Goat complained of his distressing cries, and said, "he often handles us, and we do not cry out." To this he replied, "Your handling and mine are very different things. He catches you only for your wool, or your milk, but he lays hold on me for my very life."

THE BOY AND THE FILBERTS.

A Boy put his hand into a pitcher full of filberts. He grasped as many as he could possibly hold, but when he endeavored to pull out his hand, he was prevented from doing so by the neck of the pitcher. Unwilling to lose his filberts, and yet unable to withdraw his hand, he burst into tears, and bitterly lamented his disappointment. A bystander said to him, "Be satisfied with half the quantity, and you will readily draw out your hand."

Do not attempt too much at once.

THE LABORER AND THE SNAKE.

A SNAKE, having made his hole close to the porch of a cottage, inflicted a severe bite on the Cottager's infant son, of which he died, to the great grief of his parents. The father resolved to kill the Snake, and the next day, on its coming out of its hole for food, took up his axe; but, making too much haste to hit him as he wriggled away, missed his head, and cut off only the end of his tail. After some time the Cottager, afraid lest the Snake should bite him also, endeavored to make peace, and placed some bread and salt in his hole. The Snake, slightly hissing, said: "There can henceforth be no peace between us; for whenever I see you I shall remember the loss of my tail, and whenever you see me you will be thinking of the death of your son."

No one truly forgets injuries in the presence of him who caused the injury.

THE ASS AND THE MULE.

A MULETEER set forth on a journey, driving before him an Ass and a Mule, both well laden. The Ass, as long as he traveled along the plain, carried his load with ease; but when he began to ascend the steep path of the mountain, he felt his load to be more than he could bear. He entreated his companion to relieve him of a small portion, that he might carry home the rest; but the mule paid no attention to the request. The Ass shortly afterwards fell down dead under his burden. The Muleteer, not knowing what else to do in so wild a region, placed upon the Mule the load carried by the Ass in addition to his own, and at the top of all placed the hide of the Ass, after he had flayed him. The Mule, groaning beneath his heavy burden, said thus to himself: "I am treated according to my deserts. If I had only been willing to assist the Ass a little in his need, I should not now be bearing, together with his burden, himself as well."

THE HORSE AND GROOM.

A GROOM used to spend whole days in currycombing and rubbing down his Horse, but at the same time stole his oats, and sold them for his own profit. "Alas!" said the Horse, "if you really wish me to be in good condition, you should groom me less, and feed me more."

Honesty is the best policy.

THE ASS AND THE LAP-DOG.

A MAN had an Ass, and a Maltese Lap-dog, a very great beauty. The Ass was left in a stable, and had plenty of oats and hay to eat, just as any other Ass would. The Lap-dog knew many tricks, and was a great favorite with his master, who often fondled him, and seldom went out to dine or to sup without bringing him home some tit-bit to eat, when he frisked and jumped about him in a manner pleasant to see. The Ass, on the contrary, had much work to do, in grinding the corn-mill, and in carrying wood from the forest or burdens from the farm. He often lamented his own hard fate, and contrasted it with the luxury and idleness of the Lap-dog, till at last one day he broke his cords and halter, and galloped into his master's house, kicking up his heels without measure, and frisking and fawning as well as he could. He next tried to jump about his master as he had seen the Lap-dog do, but he broke the table and smashed all the dishes upon it to atoms. He then attempted to lick his master, and jumped upon his back. The servants hearing the strange hubbub, and perceiving the danger of their master, quickly relieved him, and drove out the Ass to his stable, with kicks, and clubs, and cuffs. The Ass, as he returned to his stall beaten nearly to death, thus lamented: "I have brought it all on myself! Why could I not have been contented to labor with my companions, and not wish to be idle all the day like that useless little Lap-dog!"

THE OXEN AND THE BUTCHERS.

THE OXEN once on a time sought to destroy the Butchers, who practiced a trade destructive to their race. They assembled on a certain day to carry out their purpose, and sharpened their horns for the contest. One of them, an exceedingly old one (for many a field had he ploughed), thus spoke: "These Butchers, it is true, slaughter us, but they do so with skilful hands, and with no unnecessary pain. If we get rid of them, we shall fall into the hands of unskilful operators, and thus suffer a double death: for you may be assured, that though all the Butchers should perish, yet will men néver want beef."

Do not be in a hurry to change one evil for another.

THE LION, THE MOUSE, AND THE FOX.

A Lion, fatigued by the heat of a summer's day, fell fast asleep in his den. A Mouse ran over his mane and ears, and woke him from his slumbers. He rose up and shook himself in great wrath, and searched every corner of his den to find the Mouse. A Fox seeing him, said: "A fine Lion you are to be frightened of a Mouse." "'Tis not the Mouse I fear," said the Lion; "I resent his familiarity and ill-breeding."

Little liberties are great offences.

THE SHEPHERD'S BOY AND WOLF.

A Shepherd-boy, who watched a flock of sheep near a village, brought out the villagers three or four times by crying out, "Wolf! Wolf!" and when his neighbors came to help him, laughed at them for their pains. The Wolf, however, did truly come at last. The Shepherd-boy, now really alarmed, shouted in an agony of terror: "Pray, do come and help me; the Wolf is killing the sheep;" but no one paid any heed to his cries, nor rendered any assistance. The Wolf, having no cause of fear, took it easily, and lacerated or destroyed the whole flock.

There is no believing a liar, even when he speaks the truth.

THE MISCHIEVOUS DOG.

A Dog used to run up quietly to the heels of every-one he met, and to bite them without notice. His master suspended a bell about his neck, that he might give notice of his presence wherever he went. The Dog grew proud of his bell, and went tinkling it all over the market-place. An old hound said to him: "Why do you make such an exhibition of yourself? That bell that you carry is not, believe me, any order of merit, but, on the contrary a mark of disgrace, a public notice to all men to avoid you as an ill-mannered dog."

Notoriety is often mistaken for fame.

THE BOYS AND THE FROGS.

Some boys, playing near a pond, saw a number of Frogs in the water, and began to pelt them with stones. They killed several of them, when one of the Frogs, lifting his head out of the water, cried out: "Pray stop, my boys: what is sport to you, is death to us."

—

THE SALT MERCHANT AND HIS ASS.

A Pedlar, dealing in salt, drove his Ass to the sea-shore to buy salt. His road home lay across a stream, in passing which his Ass, making a false step, fell by accident into the water, and rose up again with his load considerably lighter, as the water melted the salt. The Pedlar retraced his steps, and refilled his panniers with a larger quantity of salt than before. When he came again to the stream, the Ass fell down on purpose in the same spot, and, regaining his feet with the weight of his load much diminished, brayed triumphantly as if he had obtained what he desired. The Pedlar saw through his trick, and drove him for the third time to the coast, where he bought a cargo of sponges instead of salt. The Ass, again playing the knave, when he reached the stream, fell down on purpose, when the sponges becoming swollen with the water, his load was very greatly increased; and thus his trick recoiled on himself in fitting to his back a double burden.

THE SICK STAG.

A SICK Stag lay down in a quiet corner of its pasture-ground. His companions came in great numbers to inquire after his health, and each one helped himself to a share of the food which had been placed for his use; so that he died, not from his sickness, but from the failure of the means of living.

Evil companions bring more hurt than profit.

THE GOATHERD AND THE WILD GOATS.

A GOATHERD, driving his flock from their pasture at eventide, found some wild goats mingled among them, and shut them up together with his own for the night. On the morrow it snowed very hard, so that he could not take the herd to their usual feeding places, but was obliged to keep them in the fold. He gave his own goats just sufficient food to keep them alive, but fed the strangers more abundantly, in the hope of enticing them to stay with him, and of making them his own. When the thaw set in, he led them all out to feed, and the wild goats scampered away as fast as they could to the mountains. The Goatherd taxed them with their ingratitude in leaving him, when during the storm he had taken more care of them than of his own herd. One of them turning about said to him, "That is the very reason why we are so cautious; for if you yesterday treated us better than the Goats you have had so long, it is plain also that if others came after us, you would in the same manner, prefer them to ourselves."

Old friends cannot with impunity be sacrificed for new ones.

THE BOY AND THE NETTLES.

A Boy was stung by a Nettle. He ran home and told his mother, saying, "Although it pains me so much, I did but touch it ever so gently." "That was just it," said his mother, "which caused it to sting you. The next time you touch a Nettle, grasp it boldly, and it will be soft as silk to your hand, and not in the least hurt you."

Whatever you do, do with all your might.

THE FOX WHO HAD LOST HIS TAIL.

A Fox caught in a trap, escaped with the loss of his "brush." Henceforth feeling his life a burden from the shame and ridicule to which he was exposed, he schemed to bring all the other Foxes into a like condition with himself, that in the common loss he might the better conceal his own deprivation. He assembled a good many Foxes, and publicly advised them to cut off their tails, saying "that they would not only look much better without them, but that they would get rid of the weight of the brush, which was a very great inconvenience." One of them interrupting him said, "If you had not yourself lost your tail, my friend, you would not thus counsel us,"

THE MAN AND HIS TWO SWEETHEARTS.

A MIDDLE-AGED man, whose hair had begun to turn grey, courted two women at the same time. One of them was young; and the other well advanced in years. The elder woman, ashamed to be courted by a man younger than herself, made a point, whenever her admirer visited her, to pull out some portion of his black hairs. The younger, on the contrary, not wishing to become the wife of an old man, was equally zealous in removing every grey hair she could find. Thus it came to pass, that between them both he very soon found that he had not a hair left on his head.

Those who seek to please everybody please nobody.

THE ASTRONOMER.

AN Astronomer used to go out of a night to observe the stars. One evening, as he wandered through the suburbs with his whole attention fixed on the sky, he fell unawares into a deep well. While he lamented and bewailed his sores and bruises, and cried loudly for help, a neighbor ran to the well, and learning what had happened said: "Hark ye, old fellow, why, in striving to pry into what is in heaven do you not manage to see what is on earth?"

THE VAIN JACKDAW.

Jupiter determined, it is said, to create a sovereign over the birds; and made proclamation that, on a certain day, they should all present themselves before him, when he would himself choose the most beautiful among them to be king. The Jackdaw, knowing his own ugliness, searched through the woods and fields, and collected the feathers which had fallen from the wings of his companions, and stuck them in all parts of his body, hoping thereby to make himself the most beautiful of all. When the appointed day arrived, and the birds had assembled before Jupiter, the Jackdaw also made his appearance in his many-feathered finery. On Jupiter proposing to make him king, on account of the

beauty of his plumage, the birds indignantly pro-
tested, and each plucking from him his own feathers,
the Jackdaw was again nothing but a Jackdaw.

THE WOLVES AND THE SHEEP.

"WHY should there always be this internecine and
implacable warfare between us?" said the Wolves
to the Sheep. "Those evil-disposed Dogs have much
to answer for. They always bark whenever we approach you, and attack us before we have done any
harm. If you would only dismiss them from your
heels, there might soon be treaties of peace and of
reconciliation between us." The sheep, poor silly
creatures! were easily beguiled, and dismissed the
Dogs. The Wolves destroyed the unguarded flock
at their own pleasure.

THE CAT AND THE BIRDS.

A CAT, hearing that the Birds in a certain aviary
were ailing, dressed himself up as a physician, and,
taking with him his cane and the instruments becoming his profession, went to the aviary, knocked
at the door, and inquired of the inmates how they
all did, saying that if they were ill, he would be
happy to prescribe for them and cure them. They
replied, "We are all very well, and shall continue
so, if you will only be good enough to go away, and
leave us as we are,"

THE KID AND THE WOLF.

A KID standing on the roof of a house, out of
harm's way, saw a Wolf passing by: and immediately began to taunt and revile him. The Wolf,
looking up, said: "Sirrah! I hear thee: yet it is not

thou who mockest me, but the roof on which thou art standing."

Time and place often give the advantage to the weak over the strong.

THE FARMER AND HIS SONS.

A FARMER being on the point of death wished to ensure from his sons the same attention to his farm as he had himself given it. He called them to his bedside, and said, "My sons, there is a great treasure hid in one of my vineyards." The sons after his death took their spades and mattocks, and carefully dug over every portion of their land. They found no treasure, but the vines repaid their labor by an extraordinary and superabundant crop.

THE HEIFER AND THE OX.

A HEIFER saw an Ox hard at work harnessed to a plough, and tormented him with reflections on his unhappy fate in being compelled to labor. Shortly afterwards, at the harvest home, the owner released the Ox from his yoke, but bound the Heifer with cords, and led him away to the altar to be slain in honor of the festival. The Ox saw what was being done, and said with a smile to the Heifer: "For this you were allowed to live in idleness, because you were presently to be sacrificed."

THE OX AND THE FROG.

An Ox drinking at a pool, trod on a brood of young frogs, and crushed one of them to death. The mother coming up, and missing one of her sons, inquired of his brothers what had become of him. "He is dead, dear mother; for just now a very huge beast with four great feet came to the pool, and crushed him to death with his cloven heel." The Frog, puffing herself out, inquired, "if the beast was as big as that in size." "Cease, mother, to puff yourself out," said her son, "and do not be angry; for you would, I assure you, sooner burst than successfully imitate the hugeness of that monster."

THE OLD WOMAN AND THE PHYSICIAN.

An old woman having lost the use of her eyes, called in a Physician to heal them, and made this bargain with him in the presence of witnesses: that if he should cure her blindness, he should receive from her a sum of money; but if her infirmity remained, she should give him nothing. This agreement being entered into, the Physician, time after time, applied his salve to her eyes, and on every visit taking something away, stole by little and little all her property: and when he had got all she had, he healed her, and demanded the promised payment. The old woman, when she recovered her sight and saw none of her goods in her house, would give him nothing. The Physician insisted on his claim, and, as she still refused, summoned her before the Archons. The old woman standing up in the Court thus spoke:— "This man here speaks the truth in what he says; for I did promise to give him a sum of money, if I should recover my sight: but if I continued blind, I was to give him nothing. Now he declares 'that I am healed.' I on the contrary affirm 'that I am still blind;' for when I lost the use of my eyes, I saw in my house various chattels and valuable goods: but now, though he swears I am cured of my blindness, I am not able to see a single thing in it."

THE FIGHTING COCKS AND THE EAGLE.

Two Game Cocks were fiercely fighting for the mastery of the farm-yard. One at last put the other to flight. The vanquished Cock skulked away and hid himself in a quiet corner. The conqueror, flying up to a high wall, flapped his wings and crowed exultingly with all his might. An Eagle sailing through the air pounced upon him, and carried him off in his talons. The vanquished Cock immediately came out of his corner, and ruled henceforth with undisputed mastery.

Pride goes before destruction.

THE CHARGER AND THE MILLER.

A CHARGER, feeling the infirmities of age, betook him to a mill instead of going out to battle. But when he was compelled to grind instead of serving in the wars, he bewailed his change of fortune, and called to mind his former state, saying, "Ah! Miller, I had indeed to go a campaigning before, but I was barbed from counter to tail, and a man went along to groom me; and now, I cannot tell what ailed me to prefer the mill before the battle." "Forbear,' said the Miller to him, "harping on what was of yore, for it is the common lot of mortals to sustain the ups and downs of fortune."

THE FOX AND THE MONKEY.

A MONKEY once danced in an assembly of the Beasts and so pleased them all by his performance that they elected him their King. A Fox envying him the honor, discovered a piece of meat lying in a trap, and leading the Monkey to the place where it was, said, "that she had found a store, but had not used it, but had kept it for him as treasure trove of his kingdom, and counselled him to lay hold of it." The Monkey approached carelessly, and was caught in the trap; and on his accusing the Fox of purposely leading him into the snare, she replied, "O Monkey, and are you, with such a mind as yours, going to be King over the Beasts?"

THE HORSE AND HIS RIDER.

A HORSE Soldier took the utmost pains with his
charger. As long as the war lasted, he looked upon
him as his fellow-helper in all emergencies, and fed

him carefully with hay and corn. When the war
was over, he only allowed him chaff to eat, and
made him carry heavy loads of wood, and subjected
him to much slavish drudgery and ill-treatment.

War, however, being again proclaimed, and the trumpet summoning him to his standard, the Soldier put on his charger its military trappings, and mounted, being clad in his heavy coat of mail.   The

Horse fell down straightway under the weight, no longer equal to the burden, and said to his master, " You must now e'en go to the war on foot, for you have transformed me from a Horse into an Ass; and how can you expect that I can again turn in a moment from an Ass to a Horse?"

THE BELLY AND THE MEMBERS.

The members of the Body rebelled against the Belly and said, " Why should we be perpetually engaged in administering to your wants, while you do nothing but take your rest, and enjoy yourself in luxury and self-indulgence?"   The members carried out their resolve, and refused their assistance to the Body.   The whole body quickly became debilitated, and the hands, feet, mouth, and eyes, when too late, repented of their folly.

THE VINE AND THE GOAT.

A VINE was luxuriant in the time of vintage with leaves and grapes. A Goat, passing by, nibbled its young tendrils and its leaves. The Vine addressed him, and said: "Why do you thus injure me without a cause, and crop my leaves? Is there no young grass left? But I shall not have to wait long for my just revenge; for if you now should crop my leaves, and cut me down to my root, I shall provide the wine to pour over you when you are led as a victim to the sacrifice."

JUPITER AND THE MONKEY.

JUPITER issued a proclamation to all the beasts of the forest, and promised a royal reward to the one whose offspring should be deemed the handsomest. The Monkey came with the rest, and presented, with all a mother's tenderness, a flat-nosed, hairless, ill-featured young Monkey as a candidate for the promised reward. A general laugh saluted her on the presentation of her son. She resolutely said, "I know not whether Jupiter will allot the prize to my son; but this I do know, that he is at least in the eyes of me his mother, the dearest, handsomest, and most beautiful of all."

THE WIDOW AND HER LITTLE MAIDENS.

A WIDOW woman, fond of cleaning, had two little maidens to wait on her. She was in the habit of waking them early in the morning, at cockcrow. The maidens being aggrieved by such excessive labor, resolved to kill the cock who roused their mistress so early. When they had done this, they found that they had only prepared for themselves greater troubles, for their mistress, no longer hearing the hour from the cock, woke them up to their work in the middle of the night.

THE HAWK, THE KITE,
AND
THE PIGEONS.

THE Pigeons, terrified by
the appearance of a Kite,
called upon the Hawk to
defend them. He at once

consented. When they had admitted him into the cote, they found that he made more havoc and slew a larger number of them in one day, than the Kite could pounce upon in a whole year.

Avoid a remedy that is worse than the disease.

THE DOLPHINS, THE WHALES, AND THE SPRAT.

The Dolphins and Whales waged a fierce warfare with each other. When the battle was at its height, a Sprat lifted its head out of the waves, and said that he would reconcile their differences, if they would accept him as an umpire. One of the Dolphins replied, "We would far rather be destroyed in our battle with each other, than admit any interference from you in our affairs."

THE SWALLOW, THE SERPENT, AND THE COURT OF JUSTICE.

A Swallow, returning from abroad, and ever fond of dwelling with men, built herself a nest in the wall of a Court of Justice, and there hatched seven young birds. A Serpent gliding past the nest, from its hole in the wall, ate up the young unfledged nestlings. The Swallow finding her nest empty, lamented greatly, and exclaimed: "Woe to me a stranger! that in this place where all others' rights are protected, I alone should suffer wrong."

THE TWO POTS.

A RIVER carried down in its stream two Pots, one made of earthenware, and the other of brass. The Earthen Pot said to the Brass Pot, "Pray keep at a distance, and do not come near me: for if you touch me ever so slightly, I shall be broken in pieces; and besides, I by no means wish to come near you."

Equals make the best friends.

THE SHEPHERD AND THE WOLF.

A SHEPHERD once found the whelp of a Wolf, and brought it up, and after a while taught it to steal lambs from the neighboring flocks. The Wolf having shown himself an apt pupil, said to the Shepherd, "since you have taught me to steal, you must keep a sharp look-out, or you will lose some of your own flock,"

THE CRAB AND ITS MOTHER.

A CRAB said to her son, "Why do you walk so one-sided, my child? It is far more becoming to go straightforward." The young Crab replied: "Quite true, dear mother; and if you will show me the straight way, I will promise to walk in it." The mother tried in vain, and submitted without remonstrance to the reproof of her child.

Example is more powerful than precept.

THE FATHER AND HIS TWO DAUGHTERS.

A MAN had two daughters, the one married to a gardener, and the other to a tile-maker. After a time he went to the daughter who had married the gardener, and inquired how she was, and how all things went with her. She said, "All things are prospering with me, and I have only one wish, that there may be a heavy fall of rain, in order that the plants may be well watered." Not long after he went to the daughter who had married the tile-maker, and likewise inquired of her how she fared; she replied, "I want for nothing, and have only one wish, that the dry weather may continue, and the sun shine hot and bright, so that the bricks might be dried." He said to her, "If your sister wishes for rain, and you for dry weather, with which of the two am I to join my wishes?"

THE THIEF AND HIS MOTHER.

A Boy stole a lesson-book from one of his school-fellows, and took it home to his mother. She not only abstained from beating him, but encouraged him. He next time stole a cloak and brought it to her, when she yet further commended him. The Youth, advanced to man's estate, proceeded to steal things of greater value. At last he was taken in the very act, and, having his hands bound behind him, was led away to the place of public execution. His mother followed in the crowd and violently beat her breast in sorrow, whereon the young man said, "I wish to say something to my mother in her ear." She came close to him, when he quickly seized her ear with his teeth and bit it off. The mother up-braided him as an unnatural child, whereon he replied, "Ah! if you had beaten me, when I first stole and brought to you that lesson-book, I should not have come to this, nor have been thus led to a disgraceful death."

THE OLD MAN AND DEATH.

An old man was employed in cutting wood in the forest, and, in carrying the faggots into the city for sale one day, being very wearied with his long journey, he sat down by the wayside, and, throwing down his load, besought "Death" to come. "Death" immediately appeared, in answer to his summons, and asked for what reason he had called him. The old man replied, "That, lifting up the load, you may place it again upon my shoulders."

THE FIR TREE AND THE BRAMBLE.

A Fir Tree said boastingly to the Bramble, "You are useful for nothing at all; while I am everywhere used for roofs and houses." The Bramble made answer: "You poor creature, if you would only call to mind the axes and saws which are about to hew you down, you would have reason to wish that you had grown up a Bramble, not a Fir Tree."

Better poverty without care, than riches with,

THE WOLF AND THE SHEEP.

A WOLF, sorely wounded and bitten by dogs, lay sick and maimed in his lair. Being in want of food, he called to a Sheep, who was passing, and asked him to fetch some water from a stream flowing close beside him. "For," he said, "if you will bring me drink, I will find means to provide myself with meat." "Yes," said the Sheep, "if I should bring you the draught, you would doubtless make me provide the meat also."

Hypocritical speeches are easily seen through,

THE MAN BITTEN BY A DOG.

A Man who had been bitten by a Dog, went about in quest of some one who might heal him. A friend meeting him, and learning what he wanted, said, "If you would be cured, take a piece of bread, and dip it in the blood from your wound, and go and give it to the Dog that bit you." The man who had been bitten, laughed at this advice, and said, "Why? If I should do so, it would be as if I should pray every Dog in the town to bite me."

Benefits bestowed upon the evil-disposed, increase their means of injuring you.

THE HUNTSMAN AND THE FISHERMAN.

A Huntsman, returning with his dogs from the field, fell in by chance with a Fisherman, bringing home a basket well ladened with fish. The Huntsman wished to have the fish; and their owner experienced an equal longing for the contents of the game-bag. They quickly agreed to exchange the produce of their day's sport. Each was so well pleased with his bargain, that they made for some time the same exchange day after day. A neighbor said to them, "If you go on in this way, you will soon destroy, by frequent use, the pleasure of your exchange, and each will again wish to retain the fruits of his own sport."

Abstain and enjoy.

THE FOX AND THE CROW.

A Crow having stolen a bit of flesh, perched in a tree, and held it in her beak. A Fox seeing her, longed to possess himself of the flesh: and by a wily stratagem succeeded. "How handsome is the Crow," he exclaimed, "in the beauty of her shape and in the fairness of her complexion! Oh, if her voice were only equal to her beauty, she would deservedly be considered the Queen of Birds!" This he said deceitfully; but the Crow, anxious to refute the reflection cast upon her voice, set up a loud caw, and dropped the flesh. The Fox quickly picked it up, and thus addressed the crow: "My good Crow, your voice is right enough, but your wit is wanting."

THE TWO DOGS.

A Man had two dogs; a Hound, trained to assist him in his sports, and a House-dog, taught to watch the house. When he returned home after a good day's sport, he always gave the House-dog a large share of his spoil. The Hound, feeling much aggrieved at this reproached his companion, saying, "It is very hard to have all this labor, while you, who do not assist in the chase, luxuriate on the fruits of my exertions." The House-dog replied, "Do not blame me, my friend, but find fault with the master, who has not taught me to labor, but to depend for subsistence on the labor of others."

Children are not to be blamed for the faults of their parents.

THE OLD WOMAN AND THE WINE-JAR.

An Old Woman found an empty jar which had lately been full of prime old wine, and which still retained the fragrant smell of its former contents. She greedily placed it several times to her nose, and drawing it backwards and forwards said, "O most delicious! How nice must the Wine itself have been when it leaves behind in the very vessel which contained it so sweet a perfume!"

The memory of a good deed lives.

THE WIDOW AND THE SHEEP.

A CERTAIN poor Widow had one solitary Sheep. At shearing time, wishing to take his fleece, and to avoid expense, she sheared him herself, but used the shears so unskilfully, that with the fleece she sheared the flesh. The Sheep, writhing with pain, said, "Why do you hurt me so, Mistress? What weight can my blood add to the wool? If you want my flesh, there is the butcher, who will kill me in a trice; but if you want my fleece and wool, there is the shearer, who will shear and not hurt me."

The least outlay is not always the greatest gain.

THE WILD ASS AND THE LION.

A WILD Ass and a Lion entered into an alliance that they might capture the beasts of the forest with the greater ease. The Lion agreed to assist the Wild Ass with his strength, while the Wild Ass gave the Lion the benefit of his greater speed. When they had taken as many beasts as their necessities required, the Lion undertook to distribute the prey, and for this purpose divided it into three shares. "I will take the first share," he said, "because I am King: and the second share, as a partner with you in the chase: and the third share (believe me) will be a source of great evil to you, unless you willingly resign it to me, and set off as fast as you can."

Might makes right.

THE STAG IN THE OX-STALL.

A Stag, hardly pressed by the hounds, and blind through fear to the danger he was running into, took shelter in a farm-yard, and hid himself in a shed among the oxen. An Ox gave him this kindly warning: "O unhappy creature! why should you thus, of your own accord, incur destruction, and trust yourself in the house of your enemy?" The Stag replied: "Do you only suffer me, friend, to stay where I am, and I will undertake to find some favorable opportunity of effecting my escape." At the approach of the evening the herdsman came to feed his cattle, but did not see the Stag; and even the farm-bailiff, with several laborers, passed through the shed, and failed to notice him. The Stag, congratulating himself on his safety, began to express his sincere thanks to the Oxen who had kindly afforded him help in the hour of need. One of them again answered him: "We indeed wish you well, but the danger is not over. There is one other yet to pass through the shed, who has as it were a hundred eyes, and, until he has come and gone, your life is still in peril." At that moment the master himself entered, and having had to complain that his oxen had not been properly fed, he went up to their racks, and cried out: "Why is there such a scarcity of fodder? There is not half enough straw for them to lie on. Those lazy fellows have not even swept the cobwebs away." While he thus examined everything in turn, he spied the tips of the antlers of the Stag peeping out of the straw. Then summoning his laborers, he ordered that the Stag should be seized, and killed.

THE PLAYFUL ASS.

An Ass climbed up to the roof of a building, and, frisking about there, broke in the tiling. The owner went up after him, and quickly drove him down, beating him severely with a thick wooden cudgel. The Ass said, "Why, I saw the Monkey do this very thing yesterday, and you all laughed heartily, as if it afforded you very great amusement."

Those who do not know their right place must be taught it.

THE EAGLE AND THE ARROW.

An Eagle sat on a lofty rock, watching the movements of a Hare, whom he sought to make his prey. An archer who saw him from a place of concealment, took an accurate aim, and wounded him mortally. The Eagle gave one look at the arrow that had entered his heart, and saw in that single glance that its feathers had been furnished by himself. "It is a double grief to me," he exclaimed, "that I should perish by an arrow feathered from my own wings."

A consciousness of misfortunes arising from a man's own misconduct aggravates their bitterness.

THE SICK KITE.

A Kite, sick unto death, said to his mother: "O Mother! do not mourn, but at once invoke the gods that my life may be prolonged." She replied, "Alas! my son, which of the gods do you think will pity you? Is there one whom you have not outraged by filching from their very altars a part of the sacrifice offered up to them?"

We must make friends in prosperity, if we would have their help in adversity.

THE LION AND THE DOLPHIN.

A Lion roaming by the sea-shore, saw a Dolphin lift up its head out of the waves, and asked him to contract an alliance with him; saying that of all the animals they ought to be the best friends, since the one was the king of beasts on the earth, and the other was the sovereign ruler of all the inhabitants of the ocean. The Dolphin gladly consented to this request. Not long afterwards the Lion had a combat with a wild bull, and called on the Dolphin to help him. The Dolphin, though quite willing to give him assistance, was unable to do so, as he could not by any means reach the land. The Lion abused him as a traitor. The Dolphin replied, "Nay, my friend, blame not me, but Nature, which, while giving me the sovereignty of the sea, has quite denied me the power of living upon the land."

THE LION AND THE BOAR.

ON a summer day, when the great heat induced a general thirst, a Lion and a Boar came at the same moment to a small well to drink. They fiercely disputed which of them should drink first, and were soon engaged in the agonies of a mortal combat. On their stopping on a sudden to take breath for the fiercer renewal of the strife, they saw some Vultures waiting in the distance to feast on the one which should fall first. They at-once made up their quarrel, saying, "It is better for us to make friends, than to become the food of Crows or Vultures,"

THE MICE AND THE WEASELS.

THE Weasels and the Mice waged a perpetual warfare with each other, in which much blood was shed. The Weasels were always the victors. · The Mice thought that the cause of their frequent defeats was, that they had not leaders set apart from the general army to command them, and that they were exposed to dangers from want of discipline. They chose therefore such mice as were most renowned for their family descent, strength, and counsel, as well as most noted for their courage in the fight, that they might marshal them in battle array, and form them into troops, regiments and battalions. When all this was done, and the army disciplined, and the herald Mouse had duly proclaimed war by challenging the Weasels, the newly chosen generals bound their heads with straws, that they might be more conspicuous to all their troops. Scarcely had the battle commenced, when a great rout overwhelmed the Mice, who scampered off as fast as they could to their holes. The generals not being able to get in on account of the ornaments on their heads, were all captured and eaten by the Weasels.

The more honor the more danger.

THE ONE-EYED DOE.

A Doe, blind of an eye, was accustomed to graze as near to the edge of the cliff as she possibly could, in the hope of securing her greater safety. She turned her sound eye towards the land, that she might get the earliest 'tidings of the approach of hunter or hound, and her injured eye towards the sea, from which she entertained no anticipation of danger. Some boatmen sailing by, saw her, and taking a successful aim, mortally wounded her. Yielding up her breath, she gasped forth this lament: "O wretched creature that I am! to take such precaution against the land, and after all to find this sea-shore, to which I had come for safety, so much more perilous,"

THE SHEPHERD AND THE SEA.

A Shepherd, keeping watch over his sheep near the shore, saw the sea very calm and smooth, and longed to make a voyage with a view to traffic. He sold all his flock, and invested it in a cargo of dates and set sail. But a very great tempest coming on, and the ship being in danger of sinking, he threw all his merchandise overboard, and hardly escaped with his life in the empty ship. Not long afterwards, on some one passing by, and observing the unruffled calm of the sea, he interrupted him and said, "Belike it is again in want of dates, and therefore looks quiet."

THE ASS, THE COCK, AND THE LION.

An Ass and a Cock were in a straw-yard together, when a Lion, desperate from hunger, approached the spot. He was about to spring upon the Ass, when the Cock (to the sound of whose voice the Lion, it is said, has a singular aversion) crowed loudly, and the Lion fled away as fast as he could. The Ass observing his trepidation at the mere crowing of a Cock, summoned courage to attack him, and galloped after him for that purpose. He had run no long distance, when the Lion turning about, seized him and tore him to pieces.

False confidence often leads into danger.

THE MILK-WOMAN AND HER PAIL.

A FARMER's daughter was carrying her pail of milk from the field to the farm-house, when she fell a-musing. "The money for which this milk will be sold, will buy at least three hundred eggs. The eggs, allowing for all mishaps, will produce two hundred and fifty chickens. The chickens will become ready for market when poultry will fetch the highest price; so that by the end of the year I shall have money enough from the perquisites that will fall to my share, to buy a new gown. In this dress I will go to the Christmas junketings, when all the young fellows will propose to me, but I will toss my head, and refuse them every one." At this moment she tossed her head in unison with her thoughts, when down fell the Milk-pail to the ground, and all her imaginary schemes perished in a moment.

THE MICE IN COUNCIL.

THE Mice summoned a council to decide how they might best devise means for obtaining notice of the approach of their great enemy the Cat. Among the many plans devised, the one that found most favor was the proposal to tie a bell to the neck of the Cat, that the Mice being warned by the sound of the tinkling might run away and hide themselves in their holes at his approach. But when the Mice further debated who among them should thus "bell the Cat," there was no one found to do it.

THE WOLF AND THE HOUSE-DOG.

A WOLF, meeting with a big well-fed Mastiff, having a wooden collar about his neck, inquired of him who it was that fed him so well, and yet compelled him to drag that heavy log about wherever he went. "The master," he replied. Then said the Wolf: "May no friend of mine ever be in such a plight; for the weight of this chain is enough to spoil the appetite."

———

THE RIVERS AND THE SEA.

THE Rivers joined together to complain to the Sea, saying, "Why is it that when we flow into your tides so potable and sweet, you work in us such a change, and make us salt and unfit to drink?" The Sea, perceiving that they intended to throw the blame on him, said, "Pray cease to flow into me, and then you will not be made briny."

Some find fault with those things by which they are chiefly benefited.

THE WILD BOAR AND THE FOX.

A WILD BOAR stood under a tree, and rubbed his tusks against the trunk. A Fox passing by, asked him why he thus sharpened his teeth when there was no danger threatening from either huntsman or hound. He replied, "I do it advisedly; for it would never do to have to sharpen my weapons just at the time I ought to be using them."

To be well prepared for war is the best guarantee of peace.

THE THREE TRADESMEN.

A GREAT city was besieged, and its inhabitants were called together to consider the best means of protecting it from the enemy. A Bricklayer present earnestly recommended bricks, as affording the best materials for an effectual resistance. A Carpenter with equal energy proposed timber, as providing a preferable method of defence. Upon which a Currier stood up, and said, "Sirs, I differ from you altogether: there is no material for resistance equal to a covering of hides; and nothing so good as leather."

Every man for himself.

THE ASS CARRYING THE IMAGE.

An Ass once carried through the streets of the city a famous wooden Image, to be placed in one of its Temples. The crowd as he passed along made lowly prostration before the Image. The Ass, thinking that they bowed their heads in token of respect for himself, bristled up with pride and gave himself airs, and refused to move another step. The driver seeing him thus stop, laid his whip lustily about his shoulders, and said, "O you perverse dull-head! it is not yet come to this, that men pay worship to an Ass."

They are not wise who take to themselves the credit due to others.

THE TWO TRAVELERS AND THE AXE.

Two men were journeying together in each other's company. One of them picked up an axe that lay upon the path, and said, "I have found an axe." "Nay, my friend," replied the other, "do not say 'I,' but 'We' have found an axe." They had not gone far before they saw the owner of the axe pursuing them, when he who had picked up the axe said, "We are undone." "Nay," replied the other, "keep to your first mode of speech, my friend; what you thought right then, think right now. Say 'I,' not 'We' are undone."

He who shares the danger ought to share the prize.

THE OLD LION.

A Lion, worn out with years, and powerless from disease, lay on the ground at the point of death. A Boar rushed upon him, and avenged with a stroke of his tusks a long remembered injury. Shortly afterwards the Bull with his horns gored him as if he were an enemy. When the Ass saw that the huge beast could be assailed with impunity, he let drive at his forehead with his heels. The expiring Lion said, "I have reluctantly brooked the insults of the brave, but to be compelled to endure contumely from thee, a disgrace to Nature, is indeed to die a double death."

THE OLD HOUND.

A HOUND, who in the days of his youth and strength had never yielded to any beast of the forest, encountered in his old age a boar in the chase. He seized him boldly by the ear, but could not retain his hold because of the decay of his teeth, so that the boar escaped. His master, quickly coming up, was very much disappointed, and fiercely abused the dog. The Hound looked up, and said, "It was not my fault, master; my spirit was as good as ever, but I could not help mine infirmities. I rather deserve to be praised for what I have been, than to be blamed for what I am."

THE BEE AND JUPITER.

A Bee from Mount Hymettus, the queen of the hive, ascended to Olympus, to present to Jupiter some honey fresh from her combs. Jupiter, delighted with the offering of honey, promised to give whatever she should ask. She therefore besought him, saying, "Give me, I pray thee, a sting, that if any mortal shall approach to take my honey, I may kill him." Jupiter was much displeased, for he loved much the race of man ; but could not refuse the request on account of his promise. He thus answered the Bee : "You shall have your request; but it will be at the peril of your own life. For if you use your sting, it shall remain in the wound you make, and then you will die from the loss of it."

Evil wishes, like chickens, come home to roost.

THE MASTER AND HIS DOGS.

A certain man, detained by a storm in his country house, first of all killed his sheep, and then his goats, for the maintenance of his household. The storm still continuing, he was obliged to slaughter his yoke oxen for food. On seeing this, his Dogs took counsel together, and said, "It is time for us to be off : for if the master spare not his oxen, who work for his gain, how can we expect him to spare us?"

He is not to be trusted as a friend who illtreats his own family.

THE WOLF AND THE SHEPHERDS.

A Wolf passing by, saw some Shepherds in a hut eating for their dinner a haunch of mutton. Approaching them, he said, "What a clamor you would raise, if I were to do as you are doing!"

THE SEASIDE TRAVELERS.

Some travelers, journeying along the sea-shore, climbed to the summit of a tall cliff, and from thence looking over the sea, saw in the distance what they thought was a large ship, and waited in the hope of seeing it enter the harbor. But as the object on which they looked was driven by the wind nearer to the shore, they found that it could at the most be a small boat, and not a ship. When however it reached the beach, they discovered that it was only a large fagot of sticks, and one,of them said to his companions, " We have waited for no purpose, for after all there is nothing to see but a fagot."

Our mere anticipations of life outrun its realities.

THE BRAZIER AND HIS DOG.

A Brazier had a little Dog, which was a great favorite with his master, and his constant companion. While he hammered away at his metals the Dog slept; but when, on the other hand, he went to dinner, and began to eat, the Dog woke up, and wagged his tail, as if he would ask for a share of his meal. His master one day, pretending to be angry, and shaking his stick at him, said, "You wretched little sluggard! what shall I do to you? While I am hammering on the anvil, you sleep on the mat; and when I begin to eat after my toil, you wake up, and wag your tail for food. Do you not know that labor is the source of every blessing, and that none but those who work are entitled to eat?"

THE ASS AND HIS SHADOW.

A TRAVELER hired an Ass to convey him to a distant place. The day being intensely hot, and the sun shining in its strength, the traveler stopped to rest, and sought shelter from the heat under the Shadow of the Ass. As this afforded only protection for one, and as the traveler and the owner of the Ass both claimed it, a violent dispute arose between them as to which of them had the right to it. The owner maintained that he had let the Ass only, and not his Shadow. The traveler asserted that he had, with the hire of the Ass, hired his Shadow also. The quarrel proceeded from words to blows, and while the men fought the Ass galloped off.

.In quarreling about the shadow we often lose the substance.

THE ASS AND HIS MASTERS.

An Ass belonging to a herb-seller, who gave him too litle food and too much work, made a petition to Jupiter that he would release him from his present service and provide him with another master. Jupiter, after warning him that he would repent his request, caused him to be sold to a tile-maker. Shortly afterwards, finding that he had heavier loads to carry, and harder work in the brick-field, he petitioned for another change of master. Jupiter, telling him that it should be the last time that he could grant his request, ordained that he should be sold to a tanner. The Ass, finding that he had fallen into worse hands, and noting his master's occupation, said, groaning: "It would have been better for me to have been either starved by the one, or to have been overworked by the other of my former masters, than to have been bought by my present owner, who will even after I am dead tan my hide, and make me useful to him."

THE OAK AND THE REEDS.

A VERY large Oak was uprooted by the wind, and thrown across a stream. It fell among some Reeds, which it thus addressed: "I wonder how you, who are so light and weak, are not entirely crushed by these strong winds." They replied, "You fight and contend with the wind, and consequently you are destroyed; while we on the contrary bend before the least breath of air, and therefore remain unbroken, and escape."

Stoop to conquer.

THE LION IN A FARM-YARD.

A Lion entered a farm-yard. The farmer, wishing to catch him, shut the gate. The Lion, when he found that he could not escape, flew upon the sheep, and killed them, and then attacked the oxen. The farmer, beginning to be alarmed for his own safety, opened the gate, when the Lion got off as fast as he he could. On his departure the farmer greviously lamented the destruction of his sheep and oxen; when his wife, who had been a spectator of all that took place, said, "On my word, you are rightly served; for how could you for a moment think of shutting up a Lion along with you in the farm-yard, when you know that you shake in your shoes if you only hear his roar at ever so great a distance?"

MERCURY AND THE SCULPTOR.

Mercury once determined to learn in what esteem he was held among mortals. For this purpose he assumed the character of a man, and visited in this disguise a Sculptor's studio. Having looked at various statues, he demanded the price of two figures of Jupiter and of Juno. When the sum at which they were valued was named, he pointed to a figure of himself, saying to the Sculptor, "You will certainly want much more for this, as it is the statue of the Messenger of the Gods, and the author of all your gain." The Sculptor replied, "Well, if you will buy these, I'll fling you that into the bargain."

THE FOX AND THE WOOD-CUTTER.

A Fox running before the hounds, came across a Wood-cutter felling an oak, and besought him to show him a safe hiding-place. The Wood-cutter advised him to take shelter in his own hut. The Fox crept in, and hid himself in a corner. The huntsman came up, with his hounds, in a few minutes, and inquired of the Wood-cutter if had seen the fox. He declared that he had not seen him, and yet pointed all the time he was speaking, to the hut where the Fox lay hid. The huntsman took no notice of the signs, but, believing his word, hastened forward in the chase. As soon as they were well away, the Fox departed without taking any notice of the Wood-cutter: whereon he called to him, and reproached him, saying, " You ungrateful fellow, you owe your life to me, and yet you leave me without a word of thanks." The Fox replied, "Indeed, I should have thanked you most fervently, if your deeds had been as good as your words, and if your hands had not been traitors to your speech."

THE BIRDCATCHER, THE PARTRIDGE, AND THE COCK.

A BIRDCATCHER was about to sit down to a dinner of herbs, when a friend unexpectedly came in. The bird-trap was quite empty, as he had caught nothing. He proceeded to kill a pied Partridge, which he had tamed for a decoy. He entreated thus earnestly for his life: "What would you do without me when next you spread your nets? Who would chirp you to sleep, or call for you the covey of answering birds?" The Birdcatcher spared his life, and determined to pick out a fine young Cock just attaining to his comb. He thus expostulated in piteous tones from his perch: "If you kill me, who will announce to you the appearance of the dawn? Who will wake you to your daily tasks? or tell you when it is time to visit the bird-trap in the morning?" He replied, "What you say is true. You are a capital bird at telling the time of day. But I and the friend who has come in must have our dinners."

Necessity knows no law.

THE WOLF AND THE LION.

A Wolf having stolen a lamb from a fold, was carrying him off to his lair. A Lion met him in the path, and, seizing the lamb, took it from him. The Wolf, standing at a safe distance, exclaimed, "You have unrighteously taken that which was mine from me." The Lion jeeringly replied, "It was righteously yours, eh? the gift of a friend?"

THE ANT AND THE DOVE.

An Ant went to the bank of a river to quench its thirst, and, being carried away by the rush of the stream, was on the point of being drowned. A Dove sitting on a tree overhanging the water, plucked a leaf, and let it fall into the stream close to her. The Ant, climbing on to it, floated in safety to the bank. Shortly afterwards a birdcatcher came and stood under the tree, and laid his lime-twigs for the Dove, which sat in the branches. The Ant, perceiving his design, stung him in the foot. He suddenly threw down the twigs, and thereupon made the Dove take wing.

The grateful heart will always find opportunities to show its gratitude.

THE MONKEY AND THE FISHERMEN.

A MONKEY perched upon a lofty tree saw some Fishermen casting their nets into a river and narrowly watched their proceedings. The Fishermen after a while gave over fishing, and, on going home to dinner, left their nets upon the bank. The Monkey, who is the most imitative of animals, descended from the tree-top, and endeavored to do as they had done. Having handled the net, he threw it into the river, but became entangled in the meshes. When drowning, he said to himself, "I am rightly served; for what business had I who had never handled a net to try and catch fish?"

THE HARES AND THE FROGS.

THE Hares, oppressed with a sense of their own exceeding timidity, and weary of the perpetual alarm to which they were exposed, with one accord determined to put an end to themselves and their troubles, by jumping from a lofty precipice into a deep lake below. As they scampered off in a very numerous body to carry out their resolve, the Frogs lying on the banks of the lake heard the noise of their feet, and rushed helter-skelter to the deep water for safety. On seeing the rapid disappearance of the Frogs, one of the Hares cried out to his companions;

"Stay, my friends, do not do as you intended; for you now see that other creatures who yet live are more timorous than ourselves."

THE SWAN AND THE GOOSE.

A CERTAIN rich man bought in the market a Goose and a Swan. He fed the one for his table, and kept the other for the sake of its song. When the time came for killing the Goose, the cook went to take him at night, when it was dark, and he was not able to distinguish one bird from the other, and he caught the Swan instead of the Goose. The Swan, threatened with death, burst forth into song, and thus made himself known by his voice, and preserved his life by his melody.

A word in season is most precious.

THE DOE AND THE LION.

A DOE hard pressed by hunters entered a cave for shelter which belonged to a Lion. The Lion concealed himself on seeing her approach; but, when she was safe within the cave, sprang upon her, and tore her to pieces. "Woe is me," exclaimed the Doe, "who have escaped from man, only to throw myself into the mouth of a wild beast!"

In avoiding one evil care must be taken not to fall into another.

THE FISHERMAN AND THE LITTLE FISH.

A FISHERMAN who lived on the produce of his nets, one day caught a single small fish as the result of his day's labor. The fish, panting convulsively, thus entreated for his life: "O Sir, what good can I be to you, and how little am I worth? I am not yet come to my full size. Pray spare my life, and put me back into the sea. I shall soon become a large fish, fit for the tables of the rich; and then you can catch me again, and make a handsome profit of me." The fisherman replied, "I should indeed be a very simple fellow, if, for the chance of a greater uncertain profit, I were to forego my present certain gain."

THE HUNTER AND THE WOODMAN.

A Hunter, not very bold, was searching for the tracks of a Lion. He asked a man felling oaks in the forest if he had seen any marks of his footsteps, or if he knew where his lair was. "I will," he said, "at once show you the Lion himself." The Hunter, turning very pale, and chattering with his teeth from fear, replied, "No, thank you. I did not ask that; it is his track only I am in search of, not the Lion himself."

The hero is brave in deeds as well as words.

THE SWOLLEN FOX.

A Fox, very much famished, seeing some bread and meat left by shepherds in the hollow of an oak, crept into the hole and made a hearty meal. When he finished, he was so full that he was not able to get out, and began to groan and lament very sadly. Another Fox passing by, heard his cries, and coming up, inquired the cause of his complaining. On learning what had happened, he said to him, "Ah, you will have to remain there, my friend, until you become such as you were when you crept in, and then you will easily get out."

THE CAMEL AND THE ARAB.

An Arab Camel-driver having completed the lading of his Camel, asked him which he would like best, to go up hill or down hill. The poor beast replied, not without a touch of reason: "Why do you ask me? Is it that the level way through the desert is closed?"

THE MILLER, HIS SON, AND THEIR ASS.

A Miller and his son were driving their Ass to a neighboring fair to sell him. They had not gone far when they met with a troop of women collected round a well, talking and laughing. "Look there," cried one of them, "did you ever see such fellows, to be trudging along the road on foot when they might ride?" The old man hearing this quickly made his son mount the Ass, and continued to walk along merrily by his side. Presently they came up to a group of old men in earnest debate. "There," said one of them, "it proves what I was a-saying. What respect is shown to old age in these days? Do you see that idle lad riding while his old father has to walk? Get down, you young scapegrace, and let the old man rest his weary limbs." Upon this the old man made his son dismount, and got up himself. In this manner they had not proceeded far when they met a company of women and children: "Why, you lazy old fellow," cried several tongues at once, "how can you ride upon the beast, while that poor little lad there can hardly keep pace by the side of you?" The good-natured Miller immediately took up his son behind him. They had now almost reached the town.

"Pray, honest friend," said a citizen, "is that Ass your own?" "Yes," says the old man. "O, one would not have thought so," said the other, "by the way you load him. Why, you two fellows are better able to carry the poor beast than he you." "Anything to please you," said the old man ; "we can but try." So, alighting with his son, they tied the legs of the Ass together, and by the help of a pole endeavored to carry him on their shoulders over a bridge near the entrance of the town. This entertaining sight brought the people in crowds to laugh at it ; till the Ass, not liking the noise, nor the strange handling that he was subject to, broke the cords that bound him, and, tumbling off the pole, fell into the river. Upon this, the old man, vexed and ashamed, made the best of his way home again, convinced that by endeavoring to please everybody he had pleased nobody, and lost his Ass into the bargain.

THE CAT AND THE MICE.

A CERTAIN house was overrun with Mice.   A Cat, discovering this, made her way into it, and began to catch and eat them one by one.   The Mice being continually devoured, kept themselves close in their holes.   The Cat, no longer able to get at them, perceived that she must tempt them forth by some device.   For this purpose she jumped upon a peg, and suspending herself from it, pretended to be dead.   One of the Mice, peeping stealthily out, saw her, and said, "Ah, my good madam, even though you should turn into a meal-bag, we will not come near you."

THE MOUSE AND THE BULL.

A Bull was bitten by a Mouse, and, pained by the wound, tried to capture him. The Mouse first reached his hole in safety, and the Bull dug into the walls with his horns, until wearied, crouching down, he slept by the hole. The Mouse peeping out, crept furtively up his flank, and, again biting him, retreated to his hole. The Bull rising up, and not knowing what to do, was sadly perplexed. The Mouse murmured forth, "The great do not always prevail. There are times when the small and lowly are the strongest to do mischief."

THE TWO FROGS.

Two Frogs dwelt in the same pool. The pool being dried up under the summer's heat, they left it, and set out together for another home. As they went along they chanced to pass a deep well, amply supplied with water, on seeing which one of the Frogs said to the other, "Let us descend and make our abode in this well: it will furnish us with shelter and food." The other replied with greater caution, "But suppose the water should fail us, how can we get out again from so great a depth?"

Do nothing without a regard to the consequences.

THE DOG AND THE COOK.

A RICH man gave a great feast, to which he invited many friends and acquaintances. His dog availed himself of the occasion to invite a stranger dog, a friend of his, saying, "My master gives a feast; you will have unusually good cheer; come and sup with me to-night." The Dog thus invited went at the hour appointed, and seeing the preparations for so grand an entertainment, said, in the joy of his heart, "How glad I am that I came! I do not often get such a chance as this. I will take care and eat enough to last me both to-day and to-morrow." While he thus congratulated himself, and wagged his tail, as if he would convey a sense of his pleasure to his friend, the Cook saw him moving about among his dishes, and, seizing him by his fore and hind paws, bundled him without ceremony out of the window. He fell with force upon the ground, and limped away, howling dreadfully. His yelling soon attracted other street dogs, who came up to him, and inquired how he had enjoyed his supper. He replied, "Why, to tell you the truth, I drank so much wine that I remember nothing. I do not know how I got out of the house."

Uninvited guests seldom meet a welcome.

THE THIEVES AND THE COCK.

Some thieves broke into a house, and found nothing but a Cock, whom they stole, and got off as fast as they could. On arriving at home they proceeded to kill the Cock, who thus pleaded for his life: "Pray spare me; I am very serviceable to men. I wake them up in the night to their work." "That is the very reason why we must the more kill you," they replied; "for when you wake your neighbors, you entirely put an end to our business."

The safeguards of virtue are hateful to the evil disposed.

THE LION, THE BEAR, AND THE FOX.

A Lion and a Bear seized upon a kid at the same moment, and fought fiercely for its possession. When they had fearfully lacerated each other, and were faint from the long combat, they lay down exhausted with fatigue. A Fox, who had gone round them at a distance several times, saw them both stretched on the ground, and the Kid lying untouched in the middle, ran in between them, and seizing the Kid scampered off as fast as he could. The Lion and the Bear saw him, but not being able to get up, said, "Woe betide us, that we should have fought and belabored ourselves only to serve the turn of a Fox!"

It sometimes happens that one man has all the toil, and another all the profit.

THE FARMER AND THE FOX.

A Farmer, having a long spite against a Fox for robbing his poultry yard, caught him at last, and, being determined to take an ample revenge, tied some tow well soaked with oil to his tail, and set it on fire. The Fox by a strange fatality rushed to the fields of the Farmer who had captured him. It was the time of the wheat harvest; but the Farmer reaped nothing that year, and returned home grieving sorely.

THE DANCING MONKEYS.

A Prince had some Monkeys trained to dance. Being naturally great mimics of men's actions, they showed themselves most apt pupils; and, when arrayed in their rich clothes and masks, they danced as well as any of the courtiers. The spectacle was often repeated with great applause, till on one occasion a courtier, bent on mischief, took from his pocket a handful of nuts, and threw them upon the stage. The Monkeys at the sight of the nuts forgot their dancing, and became (as indeed they were) Monkeys instead of actors, and pulling off their masks, and tearing their robes, they fought with one another for the nuts. The dancing spectacle thus came to an end, amidst the laughter and ridicule of the audience.

A Sea-gull having bolted down too large a fish, burst its deep gullet-bag, and lay down on the shore to die. A Kite, seeing him, exclaimed: "You richly deserve your fate ; for a bird of the air has no business to seek its food from the sea."

Every man should be content to mind his own business.

THE PHILOSOPHER, THE ANTS, AND MERCURY.

A Philosopher witnessed from the shore the shipwreck of a vessel, of which the crew and passengers were all drowned. He inveighed against the injustice of Providence, which would for the sake of one criminal perchance sailing in the ship allow so many innocent persons to perish. As he was indulging in these reflections, he found himself surrounded by a whole army of Ants, near to whose nest he was standing. One of them climbed up and stung him, and he immediately trampled them all to death with his foot. Mercury presented himself, and striking the Philosopher with his wand, said, "And are you indeed to make yourself a judge of the dealings of Providence, who hast thyself in a similar manner treated these poor Ants?"

THE TRAVELER AND FORTUNE.

A Traveler, wearied with a long journey, lay down overcome with fatigue on the very brink of a deep well. Being within an inch of falling into the water, Dame Fortune, it is said, appeared to him, and waking him from his slumber, thus addressed him: "Good Sir, pray wake up: for had you fallen into the well, the blame will be thrown on me, and I shall get an ill name among mortals ; for I find that men are sure to impute their calamities to me, however much by their own folly they have really brought them on themselves."

Every one is more or less master of his own fate.

THE FOX AND THE LEOPARD.

THE Fox and the Leopard disputed which was the more beautiful of the two. The Leopard exhibited one by one the various spots which decorated his skin. The Fox, interrupting him, said, "And how much more beautiful than you am I, who am decorated, not in body, but in mind."

———

THE LION AND THE HARE.

A LION came across a Hare, who was fast asleep on her form. He was just in the act of seizing her, when a fine young Hart trotted by, and he left the Hare to follow him. The Hare, scared by the noise, awoke, and scudded away. The Lion was not able after a long chase to catch the Hart, and he returned to feed upon the Hare. On finding that the Hare also had run off, he said, "I am rightly served for having let go the food that I had in my hand for the chance of obtaining more."

THE PEASANT AND THE EAGLE.

A PEASANT found an Eagle captured in a trap, and, much admiring the bird, set him free. The Eagle did not prove ungrateful to his deliverer, for seeing him sit under a wall, which was not safe, he flew towards him, and snatched off with his talons a bundle resting on his head, and on his rising to pursue him he let the bundle fall again. The Peasant taking it up, and returning to the same place, found the wall under which he had been sitting fallen to the ground; and he much marvelled at the requital made him by the Eagle for the service he had rendered him.

THE IMAGE OF MERCURY AND THE CARPENTER.

A VERY poor man, a Carpenter by trade, had a wooden image of Mercury, before which he made offerings day by day, and entreated the idol to make him rich: but in spite of his entreaties he became poorer and poorer. At last, being very wroth, he took his image down from its pedestal, and dashed it against the wall: when its head being knocked off out came a stream of gold, which the Carpenter quickly picked up, and said, "Well, I think thou art altogether contradictory and unreasonable; for when I paid you honor, I reaped no benefits: but now that I maltreat you I am loaded with an abundance of riches."

THE BULL AND THE GOAT.

A Bull, escaping from a Lion, entered a cave, which some shepherds had lately occupied. A He-goat was left in it, who sharply attacked him with his horns. The Bull quietly addressed him—"Butt away as much as you will. I have no fear of you, but of the Lion. Let that monster once go, and I will soon let you know what is the respective strength of a Goat and a Bull."

It shows an evil disposition to take advantage of a friend in distress.

THE LAMP.

A Lamp soaked with too much oil, and flaring very much, boasted that it gave more light than the sun. A sudden puff of wind arising, it was immediately extinguished. Its owner lit it again, and said: "Boast no more, but henceforth be content to give thy light in silence. Know that not even the stars need to be relit."

THE LION, THE FOX, AND THE ASS.

The Lion, the Fox, and the Ass entered into an agreement to assist each other in the chase. Having secured a large booty, the Lion, on their return from the forest, asked the Ass to allot his due portion to each of the three partners in the treaty. The Ass carefully divided the spoil into three equal shares, and modestly requested the two others to make the first choice. The Lion, bursting out into a great rage, devoured the Ass. Then he requested the Fox to do him the favor to make a division. The Fox accumulated all that they had killed into one large heap, and left to himself the smallest possible morsel. The Lion said, "Who has taught you my very excellent fellow, the art of division? "You are perfect to a fraction." He replied, "I learnt it from the Ass, by witnessing his fate."

Happy is the man who learns from the misfortunes of others.

THE BALD KNIGHT.

A BALD KNIGHT, who wore a wig, went out to hunt.
A sudden puff of wind blew off his hat and wig, at
which a loud laugh rang forth from his companions.
He pulled up his horse, and with great glee joined in
the joke by saying, " What marvel that hairs which
are not mine should fly from me, when they have
forsaken even the man that owns them: with whom,
too, they were born'"

THE SHEPHERD AND THE DOG.

A SHEPHERD penning his sheep in the fold for the
night was about to shut up a wolf with them, when
his Dog perceiving the wolf said, " Master, how can
you expect the sheep to be safe if you admit a wolf
into the fold?"

THE MONKEYS AND THEIR MOTHER.

THE Monkey, it is said, has two young ones at a birth. The mother fondles one, and nurtures it with the greatest affection and care; but hates and neglects the other. It happened once on a time that the young one which was caressed and loved was smothered by the too great affection of the mother, while the despised one was nurtured and reared in spite of the neglect to which it was exposed.

The best intentions will not always ensure success.

THE OAKS AND JUPITER.

THE Oaks presented a complaint to Jupiter, saying, "We bear for no purpose the burden of life, as of all the trees that grow we are the most continually in peril of the axe." Jupiter made answer, "You have only to thank yourselves for the misfortunes to which you are exposed: for if you did not make such excellent pillars and posts, and prove yourselves so serviceable to the carpenters and the farmers, the axe would not so frequently be laid to your roots."

THE HARE AND THE HOUND.

A Hound having started a Hare from his form, after
a long run, gave up the chase.   A Goat-herd seeing
him stop, mocked him, saying, "The little one is the
best runner of the two."   The Hound replied, "You
do not see the difference between us: I was only
running for a dinner, but he, for his life."

THE OAK AND THE WOODCUTTERS.

The Woodcutters cut down a Mountain Oak, split it
in pieces, making wedges of its own branches for
dividing the trunk, and for saving their labor.   The
Oak said with a sigh, "I do not care about the blows

of the axe aimed at my roots, but I do grieve at being torn in pieces by these wedges made from my own branches."

Misfortunes springing from ourselves are the hardest to bear.

THE WASP AND THE SNAKE.

A Wasp seated himself upon the head of a Snake, and striking him unceasingly with his stings wounded him to death. The Snake, being in great torment, and not knowing how to rid himself of his enemy, or to scare him away, saw a wagon heavily laden with wood, and went and purposely placed his head under the wheels, and said, "I and my enemy shall thus perish together."

THE PEACOCK AND THE CRANE.

A Peacock spreading its gorgeous tail mocked a Crane that passed by, ridiculing the ashen hue of its plumage, and saying, "I am robed, like a king, in gold and purple, and all the colors of the rainbow; while you have not a bit of color on your wings." "True," replied the Crane; "but I soar to the heights of heaven, and lift up my voice to the stars, while you walk below, like a cock, among the birds of the dunghill."

Fine feathers don't make fine birds.

THE HEN AND THE GOLDEN EGGS.

A Cottager and his wife had a Hen, which laid every day a golden egg. They supposed that it must contain a great lump of gold in its inside, and killed it in order that they might get it, when to their surprise they found that the Hen differed in no respect from their other hens. The foolish pair, thus hoping to become rich all at once, deprived themselves of the gain of which they were day by day assured.

THE ASS AND THE FROGS.

An Ass, carrying a load of wood, passed through a pond. As he was crossing through the water he lost his footing, and stumbled and fell, and not being able to raise on account of his load, he groaned heavily. Some Frogs frequenting the pool heard his lamentation, and said, "What would you do if you had to live here always as we do, when you make such a fuss about a mere fall into the water?"

Men often bear littte grievances with less courage than they do large misfortunes.

THE CROW AND THE RAVEN.

A Crow was very jealous of the Raven, because he was considered a bird of good omen, and always attracted the attention of men, as indicating by his flight the good or evil course of future events. Seeing some travellers approaching, she flew up into a tree, and perching herself on one of the branches, cawed as loudly as she could. The travellers turned towards the sound, and wondered what it boded, when one of them said to his companion, "Let us proceed on our journey, my friend, for it is only the caw of a crow, and her cry, you know, is no omen."

Those who assume a character which does not belong to them, only make themselves ridiculous.

THE TREES AND THE AXE.

A MAN came into a forest, and made a petition to the Trees to provide him a handle for his axe. The Trees consented to his request, and gave him a young ash-tree. No sooner had the man fitted from it a new handle to his axe, than he began to use it, and quickly felled with his strokes the noblest giants of the forest. An old oak, lamenting when too late the destruction of his companions, said to a neighboring cedar, "The first step has lost us all. If we had not given up the rights of the ash, we might yet have retained our own privileges, and have stood for ages."

THE BULL, THE LIONESS, AND THE WILD-BOAR HUNTER.

A Bull finding a lion's cub asleep gored him to death with his horns. The Lioness came up, and bitterly lamented the death of her whelp. A Wild-boar Hunter seeing her distress, stood afar off, and said to her, "Think how many men there are who have reason to lament the loss of their children, whose deaths have been caused by you."

THE WOLVES AND THE SHEEP-DOGS.

The Wolves thus addressed the Sheep-dogs: "Why should you, who are like us in so many things, not be entirely of one mind with us, and live with us as brothers should? We differ from you in one point only. We live in freedom, but you bow down to, and slave for, men; who, in return for your services, flog you with whips, and put collars on your necks. They make you also guard their sheep, and while they eat the mutton throw only the bones to you. If you will be persuaded by us, you will give us the sheep, and we will enjoy them in common, till we all are surfeited." The Dogs listened favorably to these proposals, and, entering the den of the Wolves, they were set upon and torn to pieces.

THE BOWMAN AND LION.

A VERY skilful Bowman went to the mountains in search of game. All the beasts of the forest fled at his approach. The Lion alone challenged him to combat. The Bowman immediately let fly an arrow, and said to the Lion: "I send thee my messenger, that from him thou mayest learn what I myself shall be when I assail thee." The Lion, thus wounded, rushed away in great fear, and on a Fox exhorting him to be of good courage, and not to run away at the first attack, he replied: "You counsel me in vain, for if he sends so fearful a messenger, how shall I abide the attack of the man himself?"

A man who can strike from a distance is no pleasant neighbor.

THE CAMEL.

WHEN man first saw the Camel, he was so frightened at his vast size that he fled away. After a time, perceiving the meekness and gentleness of his temper, he summoned courage enough to approach him. Soon afterwards, observing that he was an animal altogether deficient in spirit, he assumed such boldness as to put a bridle in his mouth, and set a child to drive him.

Use serves to overcome dread.

THE CRAB AND THE FOX.

A CRAB, forsaking the sea-shore, chose a neighboring green meadow as its feeding ground. A Fox came across him, and being very much famished ate him up. Just as he was on the point of being eaten, he said, "I well deserve my fate; for what business had I on the land, when by my nature and habits I am only adapted for the sea?"

Contentment with our lot is an element of happiness.

THE WOMAN AND HER HEN.

A Woman possessed a Hen that gave her an egg every day. She often thought with herself how she might obtain two eggs daily instead of one, and at last, to gain her purpose, determined to give the Hen a double allowance of barley. From that day the Hen became fat and sleek, and never once laid another egg.

Covetousness overreacheth itself.

THE ASS AND THE OLD SHEPHERD.

A Shepherd watched his Ass feeding in a meadow. Being alarmed on a sudden by the cries of the enemy, he appealed to the Ass to fly with him, lest they should both be captured.   He lazily replied, "Why should I, pray? Do you think it likely the conqueror will place on me two sets of panniers?" "No," rejoined the Shepherd. "Then," said the Ass, "as long as I carry the panniers, what matters it to me whom I serve?"

In a change of government the poor change nothing beyond the name of their master.

THE KITES AND THE SWANS.

THE Kites of old time had, equally with the Swans, the privilege of song. But having heard the neigh of the horse, they were so enchanted with the sound, that they tried to imitate it; and, in trying to neigh, they forgot how to sing.

The desire for imaginary benefits often involves the loss of present blessings.

THE HARES AND THE FOXES.

THE Hares waged war with the Eagles, and called upon the Foxes to help them. They replied, "We would willingly have helped you, if we had not known who ye were, and with whom ye were fighting."

Count the cost before you commit yourselves.

THE FOX AND THE HEDGEHOG.

A Fox swimming across a rapid river was carried by the force of the current into a very deep ravine, where he lay for a long time very much bruised and sick, and unable to move. A swarm of hungry blood-sucking flies settled upon him. A Hedgehog passing by compassionated his sufferings, and inquired if he should drive away the flies that were tormenting him. "By no means," replied the Fox; "pray do not molest them." "How is this?" said the Hedgehog; "do you not want to be rid of them?" "No," returned the Fox; "for these flies which you see are full of blood, and sting me but little, and if you rid me of these which are already satiated, others more hungry will come in their place, and will drink up all the blood I have left."

THE DOG AND THE HARE.

Hound having started a Hare on the hill-side pursued her for some distance: at one time biting her with his teeth as if he would take her life, and at another time fawning upon her, as if in play with another dog. The Hare said to him, "I wish you would act sincerely by me, and show yourself in your true colors. If you are a friend, why do you bite me so hard? if an enemy, why do you fawn on me?"

They are no friends whom you know not whether to trust or to distrust.

THE BULL AND THE CALF.

A Bull was striving with all his might to squeeze himself through a narrow passage which led to his stall. A young Calf came up, and offered to go before and show him the way by which he could manage to pass. "Save yourself the trouble," said the Bull; "I knew that way long before you were born."

THE STAG, THE WOLF, AND THE SHEEP.

A Stag asked a Sheep to lend him a measure of wheat, and said that the Wolf would be his surety. The Sheep, fearing some fraud was intended, excused herself, saying, "The Wolf is accustomed to seize what he wants, and to run off; and you, too, can quickly outstrip me in your rapid flight. How then shall I be able to find you, when the day of payment comes?"

Two blacks do not make one white.

THE MULE.

A MULE, frolicsome from want of work and from overmuch corn, galloped about in a very extravagant manner, and said to himself: "My father surely was a high-mettled racer, and I am his own child in speed and spirit." On the next day, being driven a long journey, and feeling very wearied, he exclaimed in a disconsolate tone: "I must have made a mistake; my father, after all, could have been only an ass."

THE EAGLE, THE CAT, AND THE WILD SOW.

AN EAGLE had made her nest at the top of a lofty oak. A Cat, having found a convenient hole, kittened in the middle of the trunk; and a Wild Sow, with her young, had taken shelter in a hollow at its foot. The Cat resolved to destroy by her arts this chance-made colony. To carry out her design, she climbed to the nest of the Eagle, and said, "Destruction is preparing for you, and for me too, unfortunately. The Wild Sow, whom you may see daily digging up the earth, wishes to uproot the oak, that she may on its fall seize our families as food for her young." Having thus deprived the Eagle of her senses through terror, she crept down to the cave of the Sow, and said, "Your children are in great danger; for as soon as you shall go out with your litter to find food, the Eagle is prepared to pounce upon one of your little pigs." Having instilled these fears into the Sow, she went and pretended to hide herself in the hollow of the tree. When night came she went forth with silent foot and obtained food for herself and her kittens; but, feigning to be afraid, she kept a look-out all through the day. Meanwhile, the Eagle, full of fear of the Sow, sat still on the branches, and the Sow, terrified by the Eagle, did not dare to go out from her cave; and thus they each, with their families, perished from hunger, and afforded an ample provision to the Cat and her kittens.

––––––

THE CROW AND THE PITCHER.

A Crow perishing with thirst saw a pitcher, and, hoping to find water, flew to it with great delight. When he reached it, he discovered to his grief that it contained so little water that he could not possibly get at it. He tried everything he could think of to reach the water, but all his efforts were in vain. At last he collected as many stones as he could carry, and dropped them one by one with his beak into the pitcher, until he brought the water within his reach, and thus saved his life.

Necessity is the mother of invention.

THE WOLF AND THE FOX.

A VERY large and strong Wolf was born among the wolves, who exceeded all his fellow-wolves in strength, size, and swiftness, so that they gave him, with unanimous consent, the name of "Lion." The Wolf, with a want of sense proportioned to his enormous size, thought that they gave him this name in earnest, and, leaving his own race, consorted exclusively with the lions. An old sly Fox, seeing this, said, "May I never make myself so ridiculous as you do in your pride and self-conceit; for you really show like a lion among wolves, whereas in a herd of lions you are a wolf."

THE PROPHET.

A WIZARD, sitting in the market-place, told the fortunes of the passers-by. A person ran up in great haste, and announced to him that the doors of his house had been broken open, and that all his goods were being stolen. He sighed heavily, and hastened away as fast as he could run. A neighbor saw him running, and said, "Oh! you follow those? you say you can foretell the fortunes of others; how is it you did not foresee your own?"

THE FOX AND THE GRAPES.

A FAMISHED FOX saw some clusters of ripe black grapes hanging from a trellised vine. She resorted to all her tricks to get at them, but wearied herself in vain, for she could not reach them. At last she turned away beguiling herself of her disappointment and saying: "The Grapes are sour, and not ripe as I thought."

THE SERPENT AND THE EAGLE.

A Serpent and an Eagle were struggling with each other in the throes of a deadly conflict. The Serpent had the advantage, and was about to strangle the bird. A countryman saw them, and running up, loosed the coil of the Serpent, and let the Eagle go free. The Serpent, irritated at the escape of his prey, let fly his poison, and injected it into the drinking horn of the countryman. The rustic, ignorant of his danger, was about to drink, when the Eagle struck his hand with his wing, and, seizing the drinking horn in his talons, carried it up aloft.

THE TWO FROGS.

Two Frogs were neighbors. The one inhabited a deep pond, far removed from public view; the other lived in a gully containing little water, and traversed by a country road. He that lived in the pond warned his friend, and entreated him to change his residence, and to come and live with him, saying that he would enjoy greater safety from danger and more abundant food. The other refused, saying that he felt it so very hard to remove from a place to which he had become accustomed. A few days afterwards a heavy wagon passed through the gully, and crushed him to death under its wheels.

A wilful man will have his way to his own hurt.

THE HART AND THE VINE.

A HART, hard pressed in the chase, hid himself beneath the large leaves of a Vine. The huntsmen, in their haste, overshot the place of his concealment; when the Hart, supposing all danger to have passed, began to nibble the tendrils of the Vine. One of the huntsmen, attracted by the rustling of the leaves, looked back, and, seeing the Hart, shot an arrow from his bow, and killed it. The Hart, at the point of death, groaned out these words, "I am rightly served; for I ought not to have maltreated the Vine that saved me."

THE THIEF AND THE INNKEEPER.

A THIEF hired a room in a tavern, and stayed some days, in the hope of stealing something which should enable him to pay his reckoning. When he had waited some days in vain, he saw the Innkeeper dressed in a new and handsome coat, and sitting before his door. The Thief sat down beside him, and talked with him. As the conversation began to flag, the Thief yawned terribly, and at the same time howled like a wolf. The Innkeeper said, "Why do you howl so fearfully?" "I will tell you," said the Thief:" "but first let me ask you to hold my clothes, for I wish to leave them in your hands. I know not, sir, when I got this habit of yawning, nor whether these attacks of howling were inflicted on me as a judgment for my crimes, or for any other cause; but this I do know, that when I yawn for the third time, I actually turn into a wolf, and attack men." With this speech he commenced a second fit of yawning, and again howled as a wolf, as he did at first. The Innkeeper hearing his tale, and, believing what he said, became greatly alarmed, and rising from his seat, attempted to run away. The Thief laid hold of his coat, and entreated him to stop, saying, "Pray wait, sir, and hold my clothes, or I shall tear them to pieces in my fury, when I turn into a wolf." At the same moment he yawned the third time, and set up a howl like a wolf. The Innkeeper, frightened lest he should be attacked, left his new coat in his hand, and ran as fast as he could into the inn for safety. The Thief made off with his new coat, and did not return again to the inn.

Every tale is not to be believed.

THE KID AND THE WOLF.

A KID, returning without protection from the pasture, was pursued by a Wolf. He turned round, and said to the Wolf: "I know, friend Wolf, that I must be your prey; but before I die, I would ask of you one favor, that you will play me a tune, to which I may dance." The Wolf complied, and while he was piping, and the Kid was dancing, the hounds, hearing the sound, came up, and, issuing forth, gave chase to the Wolf. The Wolf, turning to the Kid, said, "It is just what I deserve; for I, who am only a butcher, should not have turned piper to please you."

THE WALNUT-TREE.

A WALNUT-TREE standing by the roadside bore an abundant crop of fruit. The passers-by broke its branches with stones and sticks for the sake of the nuts. The Walnut-tree piteously exclaimed, "O wretched me! that those whom I cheer with my fruit should repay me with these painful requitals!"

THE GNAT AND THE LION.

A GNAT came and said to a Lion, "I do not the least fear you, nor are you stronger than I am. For in what does your strength consist? You can scratch with your claws, and bite with your teeth—so can a woman in her quarrels. I repeat that I am altogether more powerful than you; and if you doubt it, let us fight and see who will conquer." The Gnat, having sounded his horn; fastened itself upon the Lion, and stung him on the nostrils and the parts of the face devoid of hair. The Lion, trying to crush him, tore himself with his claws, until he punished himself severely. The Gnat thus prevailed over the Lion, and, buzzing about in a song of triumph, flew away. But shortly afterwards he became entangled in the meshes of a cobweb, and was eaten by a spider. He greatly lamented his fate, saying, "Woe is me! that I, who can wage war successfully with the hugest beasts, should perish myself from this spider, the most inconsiderable of insects!"

THE MONKEY AND THE DOLPHIN.

A SAILOR, bound on a long voyage, took with him a Monkey to amuse him while on shipboard. As he sailed off the coast of Greece, a violent tempest arose, in which the ship was wrecked, and he, his Monkey, and all the crew were obliged to swim for their lives. A Dolphin saw the Monkey contending with the waves, and supposing him to be a man (whom he is always said to befriend), came and placed himself under him, to convey him on his back in safety to the shore. When the Dolphin arrived with his burden in sight of land not far from Athens, he demanded of the Monkey if he were an Athenian, who replied that he was, and that he was descended from one of the most noble families in that city. He then inquired if he knew the Piræus (the famous harbor of Athens). The Monkey, supposing that a man was meant, answered, that he knew him very well, and that he was an intimate friend. The Dolphin, indignant at these falsehoods, dipped the Monkey under the water, and drowned him.

THE JACKDAW AND THE DOVES.

A JACKDAW seeing some Doves in a cote abundantly provided with food, painting himself white, joined himself to them, that he might share their plentiful maintenance. The Doves as long as he was silent, supposing him to be one of themselves, admitted him to their cote; but when, one day forgetting himself, he began to chatter, they, discovering his true character, drove him forth, pecking him with their beaks. Failing to obtain food among the Doves, he betook himself again to the Jackdaws. They too, not recognizing him on account of his color, expelled him from living with them. So desiring two objects, he obtained neither.

THE HORSE AND THE STAG.

THE HORSE had the plain entirely to himself. A Stag
intruded into his domain, and shared his pasture.
The Horse desiring to revenge himself on the
stranger, requested a man, if he were willing, to help
him in punishing the Stag. The man replied, that
if the Horse would receive a bit in his mouth, and
agree to carry him, that he would contrive effectual
weapons against the Stag. The horse consented,
and allowed the man to mount him. From that hour
he found that, instead of obtaining revenge on the
Stag, he had enslaved himself to the service of man.

THE FOX AND THE MONKEY.

A Fox and a Monkey were travelling together on the same road. As they journeyed, they passed through a cemetery full of monuments. "All these monuments which you see," said the Monkey, "are erected in honor of my ancestors, who were in their day freed men, and citizens of great renown." The Fox replied, "You have chosen a most appropriate subject for your falsehoods, as I am sure none of your ancestors will be able to contradict you."

A false tale often betrays itself.

THE MAN AND HIS WIFE.

A Man had a Wife who made herself hated by all the members of his household. He wished to find out if she had the same effect on the persons in her father's house. He therefore made some excuse to send her home on a visit to her father. After a short time she returned, when he inquired how she had got on, and how the servants had treated her. She replied, "The neatherds and shepherds cast on me looks of aversion." He said, "O Wife, if you were disliked by those who go out early in the morning with their flocks, and return late in the evening, what must have been felt towards you by those with whom you passed the whole of the day!"

Straws show how the wind blows.

THE THIEF AND THE HOUSE-DOG.

A Thief came in the night to break into a house. He brought with him several slices of meat, that he might pacify the House-dog, so that he should not alarm his master by barking. As the Thief threw him the piece of meat, the Dog said, "If you think to stop my mouth, you will be greatly mistaken. This sudden kindness at your hands will only make me more watchful, lest under these unexpected favors to myself, you have some private ends to accomplish for your own benefit, and for my master's injury.

THE MAN, THE HORSE, THE OX, AND THE DOG.

A Horse, Ox, and Dog, driven to great straits by the cold, sought shelter and protection from Man. He received them kindly, lighted a fire, and warmed them. He made the Horse free of his oats, gave the Ox abundance of hay, and fed the Dog with meat from his own table. Grateful for these favors, they determined to repay him to the best of their ability. They divided for this purpose the term of his life between them, and each endowed one portion of it with the qualities which chiefly characterized himself. The Horse chose his earliest years, and endowed them with his own attributes: hence every man is in his youth impetuous, headstrong, and obstinate in maintaining his own opinion. The Ox took under his patronage the next term of life, and therefore man in his middle age is fond of work, devoted to labor, and resolute to amass wealth, and to husband his resources. The end of life was reserved to the Dog, wherefore the old man is often snappish, irritable, hard to please, and selfish, tolerant only of his own household, but averse to strangers, and to all who do not administer to his comfort or to his necessities.

THE FOX AND THE LION.

A Fox who had never yet seen a Lion, when he fell
in with him by a certain chance for the first time in
the forest, was so frightened that he was near dying

with fear.   On his meeting with him for the second
time, he was still much alarmed, but not to the same
extent as at first.   On seeing him the third time, he

so increased in boldness that he went up to him, and commenced a familiar conversation with him.

Acquaintance softens prejudices.

THE WEASEL AND THE MICE.

A Weasel, inactive from age and infirmities, was not able to catch mice as he once did. He therefore rolled himself in flour and lay down in a dark corner. A Mouse, supposing him to be food, leapt upon him, and, being instantly caught, was squeezed to death. Another perished in a similar manner, and then a third, and still others after them. A very old Mouse, who had escaped full many a trap and snare, observing from a safe distance the trick of his crafty foe, said, "Ah! you that lie there, may you prosper just in the same proportion as you are what you pretend to be!"

THE BOY BATHING.

A Boy bathing in a river was in danger of being drowned. He called out to a traveller, passing by, for help. The traveller, instead of holding. out a helping hand, stood up unconcernedly, and scolded the boy for his imprudence. "Oh, sir!" cried the youth, "prey help me now, and scold me afterwards."

Counsel, without help, is useless.

THE APES AND THE TWO TRAVELLERS.

Two men, one of whom always spoke the truth and the other told nothing but lies, were travelling together, and by chance came to the land of Apes.

One of the Apes, who had raised himself to be king, commanded them to be laid hold of, and brought before him, that he might know what was said of him among men. He ordered at the same time that all the Apes should be arranged in a long row on his right hand and on his left, and that a throne should be placed for him, as was the custom among men. After these preparations he signified his will that the two men should be brought before him, and greeted them with this salutation: "What sort of a king do I seem to you to be, O strangers?" The lying Traveller replied, "You seem to me a most mighty king." "And what is your estimate of those you see around me?" "These," he made answer, "are worthy companions of yourself, fit at least to be ambassadors and leaders of armies." The Ape and all his court, gratified with the lie, commanded a handsome present to be given to the flatterer. On this the truthful Traveller thought within himself, "If so great a reward be given for a lie, with what gift may not I be rewarded, if, according to my custom, I shall tell the truth?" The Ape quickly turned to him. "And pray how do I and these my friends around me seem to you?" "Thou art," he said, "a most excellent Ape, and all these thy companions after thy example are excellent Apes, too." The King of the Apes, enraged at hearing these truths, gave him over to the teeth and claws of his companions.

THE WOLF AND THE SHEPHERD.

A WOLF followed a flock of sheep for a long time, and did not attempt to injure one of them. The Shepherd at first stood on his guard against him, as against an enemy, and kept a strict watch over his movements. But when the Wolf, day after day, kept in the company of the sheep, and did not make the slightest effort to seize them, the Shepherd began to look upon him as a guardian of his flock rather than as a plotter of evil against it; and when occasion called him one day into the city, he left the sheep entirely in his charge. The Wolf, now that he had the opportunity, fell upon the sheep, and destroyed the greater part of the flock. The Shepherd on his return finding his flock destroyed, exclaimed: "I have been rightly served; why did I trust my sheep to a Wolf?"

THE HARES AND THE LIONS.

THE HARES harangued the assembly, and argued that all should be on an equality. The Lions made this reply: "Your words, O Hares! are good; but they lack both claws and teeth such as we have."

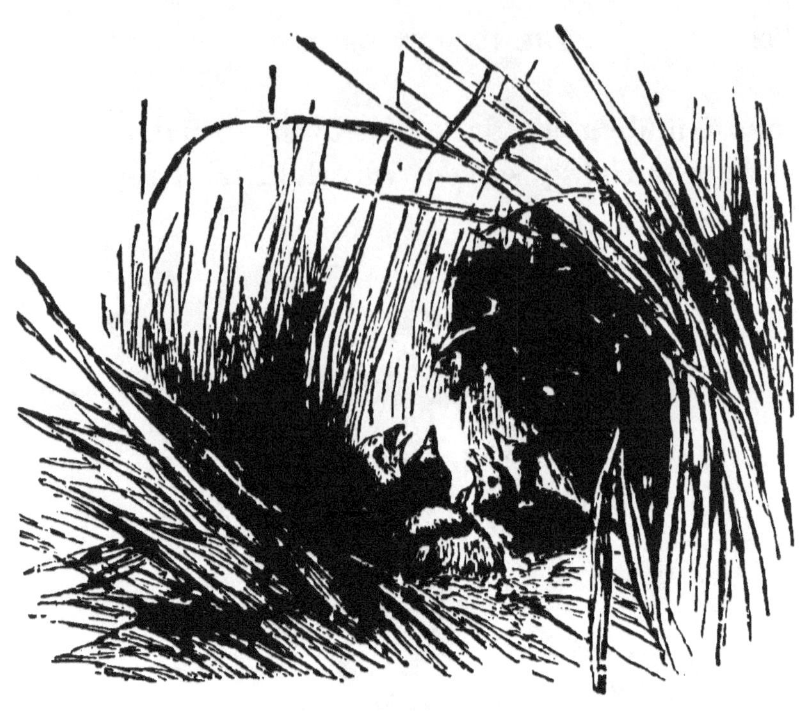

THE LARK AND HER YOUNG ONES.

A LARK had made her nest in the early spring on the young green wheat. The brood had almost grown to their proper strength, and attained the use of their wings and the full plumage of their feathers, when the owner of the field, overlooking his crop, now quite ripe, said, "The time is come when I must send to all my neighbors to help me with my harvest." One of the young Larks heard his speech, and related it to his mother, inquiring of her to what place they should move for safety. "There is no occasion to move yet, my son," she replied; "the man who only sends to his friends to help him with his harvest is not really in earnest." The owner of the field again came a few days later, and saw the wheat shedding the grain from excess of ripeness, and said, "I will come myself to-morrow with my laborers, and with as many reapers as I can hire, and will get in the harvest." The Lark on hearing these words, said to her brood, "It is time now to be off, my little ones, for the man is in earnest this time; he no longer trusts to his friends, but will reap the field himself."

Self-help is the best help.

THE PEACOCK AND JUNO.

The Peacock made complaint to Juno that, while the nightingale pleased every ear with his song, he no sooner opened his mouth than he became a laughing-stock to all who heard him. The Goddess, to console him, said, "But you far excel in beauty and size. The splendor of the emerald shines in your neck, and you unfold a tail gorgeous with painted plumage." "But for what purpose have I," said the bird, "this dumb beauty so long as I am surpassed in song?" "The lot of each," replied Juno, "has been assigned by the will of the Fates—to thee, beauty; to the eagle, strength; to the nightingale, song; to the raven, favorable, and to the crow, unfavorable, auguries. These are all contented with the endowments allotted to them."

THE ASS AND THE WOLF.

An Ass, feeding in a meadow, saw a Wolf approaching to seize him, and immediately pretended to be lame. The Wolf, coming up, inquired the cause of his lameness. The Ass said, that passing through a hedge he trod with his foot upon a sharp thorn, and requested the Wolf to pull it out, lest when he supped on him it should injure his throat. The Wolf consenting, and lifting up the foot, and giving his whole mind to the discovery of the thorn, the Ass with his heels kicked his teeth into his mouth, and galloped away. The Wolf, being thus fearfully mauled, said. "I am rightly served, for why did I attempt the art of healing, when my father only taught me the trade of a butcher?"

THE SELLER OF IMAGES.

A CERTAIN man made a wooden image of Mercury, and offered it for sale. When no one appeared willing to buy it, in order that he might attract purchasers, he cried out that he had the statue to sell of a benefactor, who bestowed wealth and helped to heap up riches. One of the bystanders said to him, "My good fellow, "why do you sell him, being such a one as you describe, when you may yourself enjoy the good things he has to give?" "Why," he replied, "I am in want of immediate help, and he is wont to give his good gifts very slowly."

THE HAWK AND THE NIGHTINGALE.

A NIGHTINGALE sitting aloft upon an oak, and singing according to his wont, was seen by a Hawk, who being in want of food, made a swoop down, and seized him. The Nightingale, about to lose his life, earnestly besought the Hawk to let him go, saying that he was not big enough to satisfy the hunger of a Hawk, who, if he wanted food, ought to pursue the larger birds. The Hawk, interrupting him, said: "I should indeed have lost my senses if I should let go food ready to my hand, for the sake of pursuing birds which are not yet even within sight."

THE DOG,
THE COCK, AND THE FOX.

A Dog and a Cock, being great friends, agreed to travel together. At nightfall they took shelter in a thick wood. The Cock, flying up, perched himself on the branches of a tree, while the Dog found a bed beneath in the hollow trunk. When the morning dawned, the Cock, as usual, crowed very loudly several times. A Fox hearing the sound, and wishing to make a breakfast on him, came and stood under the branches, saying how earnestly he desired to make the acquaintance of the owner of so magnificent a voice. The Cock, suspecting his civilities, said: "Sir, I wish you would do me the favor to go round to that hollow trunk below me, and wake up my porter, that he may open the door, and let you in." On the Fox approaching the tree, the Dog sprung out and caught him, and tore him in pieces.

THE GOAT AND THE ASS.

A MAN once kept a Goat and an Ass. The Goat envying the Ass on account of his greater abundance of food, said, "How shamefully you are treated: at one time grinding in the mill, and at another carrying heavy burdens;" and he further advised him that he should pretend to be epileptic, and fall into a ditch, and so obtain rest. The Ass gave credence to his words, and falling into a ditch, was very much bruised. His master, sending for a leech, asked his advice. He bade him pour upon the wounds the lights of a Goat. They at once killed the Goat, and so healed the Ass.

THE FOX AND THE MASK.

A Fox entered the house of an actor, and, rummaging through all his properties, came upon a Mask, an admirable imitation of a human head. He placed his paws on it, and said, "What a beautiful head! yet it is of no value, as it entirely wants brains."

THE LION AND THE BULL.

A Lion, greatly desirous of fighting a Bull, and yet afraid to attack him on account of his great size, resorted to a trick to ensure his destruction. He approached him and said, "I have slain a fine sheep, my friend; and if you will come home and partake of him with me, I shall be delighted to have your company." The Lion said this in the hope that, as the Bull was in the act of reclining to eat, he might attack him to advantage, and make his meal on him. The Bull, however, on his approach to his den, saw the huge spits and giant caldrons, and no sign whatever of the sheep, and, without saying a word, quietly took his departure. The Lion inquired why he went off so abruptly without a word of salutation to his host, who had not given him any cause of offence. "I have reasons enough," said the Bull. "I see no indication whatever of your having slaughtered a sheep, while I do see, very plainly, every preparation for your dining on a bull.

THE GRASSHOPPER AND THE OWL.

An Owl, accustomed to feed at night and to sleep during the day, was greatly disturbed by the noise of a Grasshopper, and earnestly besought her to leave off chirping. The Grasshopper refused to desist, and chirped louder and louder the more the Owl entreated. The Owl, when she saw that she could get no redress, and that her words were despised, attacked the chatterer by a stratagem. "Since I cannot sleep," she said, "on account of your song, which, believe me, is sweet as the lyre of Apollo, I shall indulge myself in drinking some nectar which Pallas lately gave me. If you do not dislike it, come to me, and we will drink it together." The Grasshopper, who was at once thirsty, and pleased with the praise of her voice, eagerly flew up. The Owl, coming forth from her hollow, seized her, and put her to death.

THE WOLF
AND
THE GOAT.

A WOLF saw a Goat feeding at the summit of a steep precipice, where he had not a chance of reaching her. He called to her, and earnestly besought her to come lower down, lest she should by some mishap get a fall; and he added that the meadows lay where he was standing, and that the herbage was most tender. She replied, "No, my friend, it is not me that you invite to the pasture, but you yourself are in want of food."

THE FOWLER AND THE VIPER.

A Fowler, taking his bird-lime and his twigs, went out to catch birds. Seeing a thrush sitting upon a tree, he wished to take it, and fitting his twigs to a proper length, he watched intently, having his whole thoughts directed towards the sky. While thus looking upwards, he unawares trod upon a Viper asleep just before his feet. The Viper, turning towards him, stung him; and he, falling into a swoon, said to himself, "Woe is me! that while I proposed to hunt another, am myself fallen unawares into the snares of death."

THE HORSE AND THE ASS.

A Horse, proud of his fine trappings, met an Ass on the highway. The Ass being heavily laden moved slowly out of the way. "Hardly," said the Horse, "can I resist kicking you with with my heels." The Ass held his peace, and made only a silent appeal to the justice of the gods. Not long afterwards the Horse, having become broken-winded, was sent by his owner to the farm. The Ass seeing him drawing a dung-cart, thus derided him: "Where, O boaster, are now all thy gay trappings, thou who art thyself reduced to the condition you so lately treated with contempt?"

THE LION AND THE THREE BULLS.

THREE BULLS for a long time pastured together. A Lion lay in ambush in the hope of making them his prey, but was afraid to attack them whilst they kept together. Having at last by guileful speeches succeeded in separating them, he attacked them without fear, as they fed alone, and feasted on them one by one at his own leisure.

Union is strength.

THE FLY AND THE DRAUGHT-MULE.

A FLY sat on the axle-tree of a chariot, and addressing the Draught-mule said, "How slow you are!
Why do you not go faster? See if I do not prick
your neck with my sting." The Draught-mule replied, "I do not heed your threats; I only care for
him who sits above you, who quickens my pace with
his whip, or holds me back with the reins. Away,
therefore, with your insolence, for I know well when
to go fast, and when to go slow."

THE FISHERMEN.

SOME Fishermen were out trawling their nets. Perceiving them to be very heavy, they danced about
for joy, and supposed they had taken a large draught
of fish. When they had dragged the nets to the
shore they found but few fish, and that the nets were
full of sand and stones, and they were beyond measure cast down—not so much at the disappointment
which had befallen them, as because they had formed
such very different expectations. One of their company, an old man, said, "Let us cease lamenting,
my mates, for, as it seems to me, sorrow is always
the twin sister of joy; and it was only to be looked
for that we, who just now were over-rejoiced, should
next have something to make us sad."

THE TOWN MOUSE AND THE COUNTRY
MOUSE.

A COUNTRY Mouse invited a Town Mouse, an intimate friend, to pay him a visit, and partake of his country fare.   As they were on the bare ploughlands, eating their wheat-stalks and roots pulled up from the hedge-row, the Town Mouse said to his friend, "You live here the life of the ants: while in my house is the horn of plenty. I am surrounded with every luxury, and if you will come with me, as I much wish you would, you shall have an ample share of my dainties." The Country Mouse was easily persuaded, and returned to town with his friend. On his arrival, the Town Mouse placed before him bread, barley, beans, dried figs, honey, raisins, and, last of all, brought a dainty piece of cheese from a basket. The Country Mouse, being much delighted at the sight of such good cheer, expressed his satisfaction in warm terms, and lamented his own hard fate. Just as they were beginning to eat, some one opened the door, and they both ran off squeaking as fast as they could to a hole so narrow that two could only find room in it by squeezing. They had scarcely again begun their repast when some one else entered to take something out of a cupboard, on which the two Mice, more frightened than before, ran away and hid themselves. At last the Country Mouse, almost famished, thus addressed his friend: "Although you have prepared for me so dainty a feast, I must leave you to enjoy it by yourself. It is surrounded by too many dangers to please me. I prefer my bare plough-lands and roots from the hedge-row, so that I only can live in safety, and without fear."

———

THE WOLF, THE FOX, AND THE APE.

A Wolf accused a Fox of theft, but he entirely denied the charge. An Ape undertook to adjudge the matter between them. When each had fully stated his case, the Ape pronounced this sentence: "I do not think you, Wolf, ever lost what you claim; and I do believe you, Fox, to have stolen what you so stoutly deny."

The dishonest, if they act honestly, get no credit.

THE GEESE
AND
THE CRANES.

THE GEESE and the Cranes fed in the same meadow. A bird-catcher came to ensnare them in his nets. The Cranes

being light of wing, fled away at his approach; while the Geese, being slower of flight and heavier in their bodies, were captured.

THE WASPS, THE PARTRIDGES, AND THE FARMER.

THE WASPS and the Partridges, overcome with thirst, came to a Farmer and besought him to give them some water to drink. They promised amply to repay him the favor which they asked. The Partridges declared that they would dig around his vines, and make them produce finer grapes. The Wasps said that they would keep guard and drive off thieves with their stings. The Farmer, interrupting them, said: "I have already two oxen, who without making any promises, do all these things. It is surely better for me to give the water to them than to you."

THE BROTHER AND THE SISTER.

A FATHER had one son and one daughter; the former remarkable for his good looks, the latter for her extraordinary ugliness. While they were playing one day as children, they happened to chance to look together into a mirror that was placed on their mother's chair. The boy congratulated himself on his good looks; the girl grew angry, and could not bear the self-praises of her Brother; interpreting all he said (and how could she do otherwise?) into reflection on herself. She ran off to her father, to be avenged in her turn on her Brother, and spitefully accused him of having, as a boy, made use of that which belonged only to girls. The father embraced them both, and bestowing his kisses and affection impartially on each, said: "I wish you both every day to look into the mirror: you, my son, that you may not spoil your beauty by evil conduct; and you, my daughter, that you may make up for your want of beauty by your virtues."

THE BLIND MAN AND THE WHELP

A Blind Man was accustomed to distinguish different animals by touching them with his hands. The whelp of a Wolf was brought him, with a request that he would feel it, and say what it was. He felt it, and being in doubt, said: "I do not quite know whether it is the cub of a Fox, or the whelp of a Wolf; but this I know full well, that it would not be safe to admit him to the sheepfold."

Evil tendencies are shown in early life.

THE DOGS AND THE FOX.

Some Dogs, finding the skin of a lion, began to tear it in pieces with their teeth. A Fox, seeing them, said, "If this lion were alive, you would soon find out that his claws were stronger than your teeth."

It is easy to kick a man that is down.

THE COBBLER TURNED DOCTOR.

A Cobbler unable to make a living by his trade, rendered desperate by poverty, began to practice medicine in a town in which he was not known. He sold a drug, pretending that it was an antidote to all poisons, and obtained a great name for himself by long-winded puffs and advertisements. He happened to fall sick himself of a serious illness, on which the Governor of the town determined to test his skill. For this purpose he called for a cup, and while filling it with water, pretended to mix poison with the Cobbler's antidote, and commanded him to drink it, on the promise of a reward. The Cobbler, under the fear of death, confessed that he had no knowledge of medicine, and was only made famous by the stupid clamors of the crowd. The Governor called a public assembly, and thus addressed the citizens: "Of what folly have you been guilty? You have not hesitated to entrust your heads to a man, whom no one could employ to make even the shoes for their feet."

THE WOLF AND THE HORSE.

A WOLF coming out of a field of oats met with a Horse, and thus addressed him: "I would advise you to go into that field. It is full of capital oats, which I have left untouched for you, as you are a friend the very sound of whose teeth it will be a pleasure to me to hear." The Horse replied, "If oats had been the food of wolves, you would never have indulged your ears at the cost of your belly."

Men of evil reputation, when they perform a good deed, fail to get credit for it.

THE TWO MEN WHO WERE ENEMIES.

Two Men, deadly enemies to each other, sailed in the same vessel. Determined to keep as far apart as possible, the one seated himself in the stern, and the other in the prow of the ship. A violent storm having arisen, and the vessel being in great danger of sinking, the one in the stern inquired of the pilot which of the two ends of the ship would go down first. On his replying that he supposed it would be the prow, then said the Man, "Death would not be grievous to me, if I could only see my Enemy die before me."

THE GAME-COCKS AND THE PARTRIDGE.

A Man had two Game-cocks in his poultry-yard. One day by chance he fell in with a tame Partridge for sale. He purchased it, and brought it home that it might be reared with his Game-cocks. On its being put into the poultry-yard they struck at it, and followed it about, so that the Partridge was grievously troubled in mind, and supposed that he was thus evilly treated because he was a stranger. Not long afterwards he saw the Cocks fighting together, and not separating before one had well beaten the other. He then said to himself, "I shall no longer distress myself at being struck at by these Game-cocks, when I see that they cannot even refrain from quarrelling with each other."

THE QUACK FROG.

A Frog once on a time came forth from his home in the marsh, and made proclamation to all the beasts that he was a learned physician, skilled in the use of drugs, and able to heal all diseases. A Fox asked him, "How can you pretend to prescribe for others, who are unable to heal your own lame gait and wrinkled skin?"

THE LION, THE WOLF, AND THE FOX.

A Lion, growing old, lay sick in his cave. All the beasts came to visit their king, except the Fox. The Wolf, therefore, thinking that he had a capital opportunity, accused the Fox to the Lion for not paying any respect to him who had the rule over them all, and for not coming to visit him. At that very moment the Fox came in, and heard these last words of the Wolf. The Lion roaring out in a rage against him, he sought an opportunity to defend himself, and said, "And who of all those who have come to you have benefited you so much as I, who have travelled from place to place in every direction, and have sought and learnt from the physicians the means of healing you?" The Lion commanded him immediately to tell him the cure, when he replied, "You must flay a wolf alive, and wrap his skin yet warm around you." The Wolf was at once taken and flayed; whereon the Fox, turning to him, said, with a smile, "You should have moved your master not to ill, but to good, will."

THE DOG'S HOUSE.

A Dog, in the winter time, rolled together and coiled up in as small a space as possible on account of the cold, determined to make himself a house. When the summer returned again he lay asleep, stretched at his full length, and appeared to himself to be of a great size, and considered that it would be neither an easy nor a necessary work to make himself such a house as would accommodate him.

THE NORTH WIND AND THE SUN.

THE North Wind and the Sun disputed which was
the most powerful, and agreed that he should be
declared the victor, who could first strip a wayfaring
man of his clothes. The North Wind first tried his
power, and blew with all his might: but the keener
became his blasts, the closer the Traveller wrapped
his cloak around him; till at last, resigning all hope
of victory, he called upon the Sun to see what he
could do. The Sun suddenly shone out with all his
warmth. The Traveller no sooner felt his genial
rays than he took off one garment after another, and

at last, fairly overcome with heat, undressed, and bathed in a stream that lay in his path.

Persuasion is better than Force.

THE CROW AND MERCURY.

A Crow caught in a snare prayed to Apollo to release him, making a vow to offer some frankincense at his shrine. Being rescued from his danger, he forgot his promise. Shortly afterwards, on being again caught in a second snare, passing by Apollo he made the same promise to offer frankincense to Mercury, when he appeared, and said to him, "O thou most base fellow! how can I believe thee, who hast disowned and wronged thy former patron?"

THE FOX AND THE CRANE.

A Fox invited a Crane to supper, and provided nothing for his entertainment but some soup made of pulse, and poured out into a broad flat stone dish. The soup fell out of the long bill of the Crane at every mouthful, and his vexation at not being able to eat afforded the Fox most intense amusement. The Crane, in his turn, asked the Fox to sup with him, and set before her a flagon, with a long narrow mouth, so that he could easily insert his neck, and enjoy its contents at his leisure; while the Fox, unable even to taste it, met with a fitting requital, after the fashion of her own hospitality.

THE WOLF AND THE LION.

A Wolf, roaming by the mountain's side, saw his own shadow, as the sun was setting, become greatly extended and magnified, and he said to himself, "Why should I, being of such an immense size, and extending nearly an acre in length, be afraid of the Lion? Ought I not to be acknowledged as King of all the collected beasts?" While he was indulging in these proud thoughts, a Lion fell upon him, and killed him. He exclaimed with a too late repentance, "Wretched me! this over-estimation of myself is the cause of my destruction."

THE BIRDS, THE BEASTS, AND THE BAT.

THE Birds waged war with the Beasts, and each party were by turns the conquerors. A Bat, fearing the uncertain issues of the fight, always betook himself to that side which was the strongest. When peace was proclaimed, his deceitful conduct was apparent to both the combatants, he was driven forth from the light of day, and henceforth concealed himself in dark hiding-places, flying always alone and at night.

THE SPENDTHRIFT AND THE SWALLOW.

A YOUNG man, a great spendthrift, had run through all his patrimony, and had but one good cloak left. He happened to see a Swallow, which had appeared before its season, skimming along a pool and twittering gaily. He supposed that summer had come, and went and sold his cloak. Not many days after, the winter having set in again with renewed frost and cold, he found the unfortunate Swallow lifeless on the ground; and said, "Unhappy bird! what have you done? By thus appearing before the spring-time you have not only killed yourself, but you have wrought my destruction also."

THE TRUMPETER TAKEN PRISONER.

A TRUMPETER, bravely leading on the soldiers, was captured by the enemy. He cried out to his captors, "Pray spare me, and do not take my life without cause or without injury. I have not slain a single man of your troop. I have no arms, and carry nothing but this one brass trumpet." "That is the very reason for which you should be put to death," they said; "for while you do not fight yourself, your trumpet stirs up all the others to battle."

THE FOX AND THE LION.

A Fox saw a Lion confined in a cage, and, standing near him, bitterly reviled him. The Lion said to the Fox, "It is not thou who revilest me; but this mischance which has befallen me."

THE OWL AND THE BIRDS.

An Owl, in her wisdom, counselled the Birds, when the acorn first began to sprout, to pull it up by all means out of the ground, and not to allow it to grow because it would produce the mistletoe, from which an irremediable poison, the bird-lime, would be extracted, by which they would be captured. The Owl next advised them to pluck up the seed of the flax, which men had sown, as it was a plant which boded no good to them. And, lastly, the Owl, seeing an archer approach, predicted that this man, being on foot, would contrive darts armed with feathers, which should fly faster than the wings of the Birds themselves. The Birds gave no credence to these warning words, but considered the Owl to be beside herself, and said that she was mad. But afterwards, finding her words were true, they wondered at her knowledge, and deemed her to be the wisest of birds. Hence it is that when she appears they resort to her as knowing all things; while she no longer gives them advice, but in solitude laments their past folly.

THE ASS IN THE LION'S SKIN.

An Ass, having put on the Lion's skin, roamed about in the forest, and amused himself by frightening all the foolish animals he met with in his wanderings. At last meeting a Fox, he tried to frighten him also, but the Fox no sooner heard the sound of his voice, than he exclaimed, "I might possibly have been frightened myself, if I had not heard your bray."

THE GOODS AND THE ILLS.

All the *Goods* were once driven out by the *Ills* from that common share which they each had in the affairs of mankind; for the *Ills* by reason of their numbers had prevailed to possess the earth. The *Goods* wafted themselves to heaven, and asked for a righteous vengeance on their persecutors. They entreated Jupiter that they might no longer be associated with the *Ills*, as they had nothing in common, and could not live together, but were engaged in unceasing warfare, and that an indissoluble law might be laid down, for their future protection. Jupiter granted their request, and decreed that henceforth the *Ills* should visit the earth in company with each other, but that the *Goods* should one by one enter the habitations of men. Hence it arises that *Ills* abound, for they come not one by one, but in troops, and by no means singly: while the *Goods* proceed from Jupiter, and are given, not alike to all, but singly, and separately; and one by one to those who are able to discern them.

THE SPARROW AND THE HARE.

A HARE pounced upon by an eagle sobbed very much, and uttered cries like a child. A Sparrow upbraided her, and said, "Where now is thy remarkable swiftness of foot? Why were your feet so slow?" While the Sparrow was thus speaking, a hawk seized him on a sudden, and killed him. The Hare was comforted in her death, and expiring said, "Ah! you who so lately, when you supposed yourself safe, exulted over my calamity, have now yourself reason to deplore a similar misfortune."

THE MAN AND THE SATYR.

A MAN and a Satyr once poured out libations together in token of a bond of alliance being formed between them.   One very cold wintry day, as they talked together, the Man put his fingers to his mouth and blew on them.   On the Satyr inquiring the reason of this, he told him that he did it to warm his hands, they were so cold.   Later on in the day they sat down to eat, the food prepared being quite scalding.   The man raised one of his dishes a little towards his mouth and blew in it.   On the Satyr again inquiring the reason of this, he said that he did it to cool the meat, it was so hot.   "I can no longer consider you as a friend," said the Satyr, "a fellow who with the same breath blows hot and cold."

THE ASS AND HIS PURCHASER.

A MAN wished to purchase an Ass, and agreed with its owner that he should try him before he bought him. He took the Ass home, and put him in the straw-yard with his other Asses, upon which he left all the others, and joined himself at once to the most idle and the greatest eater of them all. The man put a halter on him, and led him back to his owner; and on his inquiring how, in so short a time, he could have made a trial of him, "I do not need," he answered, "a trial; I know that he will be just such another as the one whom of all the rest he chose for his companion."

A man is known by the company he keeps.

THE FLEA AND THE OX.

A FLEA thus questioned the Ox: "What ails you, that, being so huge and strong, you submit to the wrongs you receive from men, and thus slave for them day by day; while I, being so small a creature, mercilessly feed on their flesh, and drink their blood without stint?" The Ox replied: "I do not wish to be ungrateful; for I am loved and well cared for by men, and they often pat my head and shoulders." "Woe's me!" said the Flea; "this very patting which you like, whenever it happens to me, brings with it my inevitable destruction."

THE DOVE AND THE CROW.

A Dove shut up in a cage was boasting of the large number of the young ones which she had hatched. A Crow hearing her, said: "My good friend, cease from this unreasonable boasting. The larger the number of your family, the greater your cause of sorrow, in seeing them shut up in this prison-house."

MERCURY AND THE WORKMEN.

A Workman, felling wood by the side of a river, let his axe drop by accident into a deep pool. Being thus deprived of the means of his livelihood, he sat down on the bank, and lamented his hard fate. Mercury appeared, and demanded the cause of his tears. He told him his misfortune, when Mercury plunged into the stream, and, bringing up a golden axe, inquired if that were the one he had lost. On his saying that it was not his, Mercury disappeared beneath the water a second time, and returned. with a silver axe in his hand, and again demanded of the Workman "if it were his." On the Workman saying it was not, he dived into the pool for the third time, and brought up the axe that had been lost. On the Workman claiming it, and expressing his joy at its recovery, Mercury, pleased with his honesty, gave him the golden and the silver axes in addition to his own.

The Workman, on his return to his house, related to his companions all that had happened. One of them at once resolved to try whether he could not also secure the same good fortune to himself. He ran to the river, and threw his axe on purpose into the pool at the same place, and sat down on the bank to weep. Mercury appeared to him just as he hoped he would; and having learned the cause of his grief, plunged into the stream, and brought up a golden axe, and inquired if he had lost it. The Workman seized it greedily, and declared that of a truth it was the very same axe that he had lost. Mercury, displeased at his knavery, not only took away the golden axe, but refused to recover for him the axe he had thrown into the pool.

THE EAGLE AND THE JACKDAW.

An Eagle flying down from his eyrie, on a lofty rock, seized upon a lamb, and carried him aloft on his talons. A Jackdaw, who witnessed the capture of the lamb, was stirred with envy, and determined to emulate the strength and flight of the Eagle. He flew round with a great whirr of his wings, and settled upon a large ram, with the intention of carrying him off, but his claws becoming entangled in his fleece he was not able to release himself, although he fluttered with his feathers as much as he could. The shepherd, seeing what had happened, ran up and caught him.   He at once clipped his wings, and taking him home at night, gave him to his children. On their saying, "Father, what kind of bird is it?" he replied, "To my certain knowledge he is a Daw; but he will have it that he is an Eagle."

JUPITER, NEPTUNE, MINERVA, AND MOMUS.

ACCORDING to an ancient legend, the first man was made by Jupiter, the first bull by Neptune, and the first house by Minerva.   On the completion of their labors, a dispute arose as to which had made the most perfect work.   They agreed to appoint Momus as judge, and to abide by his decision.   Momus, however, being very envious of the handicraft of each, found fault with all.   He first blamed the work of Neptune, because he had not made the horns of the bull below his eyes, that he might better see where to strike.   He then condemned the work of Jupiter, because he had not placed the heart of man on the outside, that every one might read the thoughts of the evil disposed, and take precautions against the intended mischief.   And, lastly, he inveighed against Minerva, because she had not contrived iron wheels in the foundation of her house, that its inhabitants might more easily remove if a neighbor should prove unpleasant.   Jupiter, indignant at such inveterate fault-finding, drove him from his office of judge, and expelled him from the mansions of Olympus.

THE EAGLE AND THE FOX.

An Eagle and a Fox formed an intimate friendship, and decided to live near each other. The Eagle built her nest in the branches of a tall tree, while the Fox crept into the underwood and there produced her young. Not long after they had agreed upon this plan, when the Fox was ranging for food, the Eagle being in want of provision for her young ones, swooped down and seized upon one of the little cubs, and feasted herself and brood. The Fox on her return, discovering what had happened, was less grieved for the death of her young than for her inability to avenge them. A just retribution, however, quickly fell upon the Eagle. While hovering near an altar, on which some villagers were sacrificing a goat, she suddenly seized a piece of the flesh, and carried with it to her nest a burning cinder. A strong breeze soon fanned the spark into a flame, and the eaglets, as yet unfledged and helpless, were roasted in their nest and dropped down dead at the bottom of the tree. The Fox gobbled them up in the sight of the Eagle.

THE TWO BAGS.

EVERY man, according to an ancient legend, is born into the world with two bags suspended from his neck—a small bag in front full of his neighbors' faults, and a large bag behind filled with his own faults. Hence it is that men are quick to see the faults of others, and yet are often blind to their own failings.

THE STAG AT THE POOL.

A STAG overpowered by heat came to a spring to drink. Seeing his own shadow reflected in the water, he greatly admired the size and variety of his horns, but felt angry with himself for having such slender and weak feet. While he was thus contemplating himself, a Lion appeared at the pool and crouched to spring upon him. The Stag immediately betook himself to flight: and exerting his utmost speed, as long as the plain was smooth and open, kept himself with ease at a safe distance from the Lion. But entering a wood he became entangled by his horns: and the Lion quickly came up with him and caught

him. When too late he thus reproached himself:
"Woe is me! How have I deceived myself! These
feet which would have saved me I despised, and I
gloried in these antlers which have proved my
destruction."

What is most truly valuable is often underrated.

THE BITCH AND HER WHELPS.

A Bitch ready to whelp, earnestly begged of a
shepherd a place where she might litter. On her
request being granted, she again besought per-
mission to rear her puppies in the same spot. The
shepherd again consented. But at last the Bitch,
protected with the body-guard of her Whelps, who
had now grown up, and were able to defend themselves, asserted her exclusive right to the place, and
would not permit the shepherd to approach.

THE DOGS AND THE HIDES.

SOME Dogs, famished with hunger, saw some cow hides steeping in a river. Not being able to reach them, they agreed to drink up the river: but it fell out that they burst themselves with drinking long before they reached the hides.

Attempt not impossibilities.

THE JACKDAW AND THE FOX.

A HALF-FAMISHED Jackdaw seated himself on a fig-tree, which had produced some fruit entirely out of season, and waited in the hope that the figs would ripen. A Fox seeing him sitting so long, and learning the reason of his doing so, said to him, "You are indeed, sir, sadly deceiving yourself; you are indulging a hope strong enough to cheat you, but which will never reward you with enjoyment."

THE LARK BURYING ITS FATHER.

THE LARK (according to an ancient legend) was created before the earth itself: and when her father died by a fell disease, as there was no earth, she could find for him no place of burial. She let him lie uninterred for five days, and on the sixth day, being in perplexity, she buried him in her own head. Hence she obtained her crest, which is popularly said to be her father's grave-hillock.

Youth's first duty is reverence to parents.

THE GNAT AND THE BULL.

A GNAT settled on the horn of a Bull, and sat there a long time. Just as he was about to fly off, he made a buzzing noise, and inquired of the Bull if he would like him to go. The Bull replied, "I did not know you had come, and I shall not miss you when you go away."

Some men are of more consequence in their own eyes than in the eyes of their neighbors.

THE MONKEY AND THE CAMEL.

THE beasts of the forest gave a splendid entertainment at which the Monkey stood up and danced. Having vastly delighted the assembly, he sat down amidst universal applause. The Camel, envious of the praises bestowed on the Monkey, and desirous to divert to himself the favor of the guests, proposed to stand up in his turn, and dance for their amusement. He moved about in so utterly ridiculous a manner, that the Beasts in a fit of indignation set upon him with clubs, and drove him out of the assembly.

It is absurd to ape our betters.

THE SHEPHERD AND THE SHEEP.

A SHEPHERD driving his Sheep to a wood, saw an oak of unusual size, full of acorns, and, spreading his cloak under the branches, he climbed up into the tree, and shook down the acorns. The Sheep eating the acorns, inadvertently frayed and tore the cloak. The Shepherd coming down, and seeing what was done, said, "O you most ungrateful creatures! you provide wool to make garments for all other men, but you destroy the clothes of him who feeds you."

THE PEASANT AND THE APPLE-TREE.

A PEASANT had in his garden an Apple-tree, which bore no fruit, but only served as a harbor for the sparrows and grasshoppers. He resolved to cut it down, and, taking his axe in his hand, made a bold stroke at its roots. The grasshoppers and sparrows entreated him not to cut down the tree that sheltered them, but to spare it, and they would sing to him and listen to his labors. He paid no attention to their request, but gave the tree a second and a third blow with his axe: when he reached the hollow of the tree, he found a hive full of honey. Having tasted the honeycomb, he threw down his axe, and, looking on the tree as sacred took great care of it.

Self interest alone moves some men.

THE TWO SOLDIERS AND THE ROBBER.

Two Soldiers travelling together, were set upon by a Robber. The one fled away; the other stood his ground, and defended himself with his stout right hand. The Robber being slain, the timid companion runs up and draws his sword, and then, throwing back his travelling cloak, says, "I'll at him, and I'll take care he shall learn whom he has attacked." On this he who had fought with the Robber made answer, "I only wish that you had helped me just now, even if it had been only with those words, for I should have been the more encouraged, believing them to be true; but now put up your sword in its sheath and hold your equally useless tongue, till you can deceive others who do not know you. I, indeed, who have experienced with what speed you ran away, know right well that no dependence can be placed on your valor."

THE TREES UNDER THE PROTECTION OF THE GODS.

THE GODS, according to an ancient legend, made choice of certain trees to be under their special protection. Jupiter chose the oak, Venus the myrtle, Apollo the laurel, Cybele the pine, and Hercules the poplar. Minerva, wondering why they had preferred trees not yielding fruit, inquired the reason of their choice. Jupiter replied, "It is lest we should seem to covet the honor for the fruit." But said Minerva, "Let any one say what he will, the olive is more dear to me on account of its fruit." Then said Jupiter, "My daughter, you are rightly called wise; for unless what we do is useful, the glory of it is vain."

TRUTH AND THE TRAVELLER.

A WAYFARING Man, travelling in the desert, met a woman standing alone and terribly dejected. He inquired of her, "Who art thou?" "My name is Truth," she replied. "And for what cause," he asked, "have you left the city, to dwell alone here in the wilderness?" She made answer, "Because in former times, falsehood was with few, but is now with all men, whether you would hear or speak."

THE MANSLAYER.

A MAN committed a murder, and was pursued by the relations of the man whom he murdered. On his reaching the river Nile he saw a Lion on its bank, and being fearfully afraid, climbed up a tree. He found a serpent in the upper branches of the tree, and again being greatly alarmed he threw himself into the river, when a crocodile caught him and ate him. Thus the earth, the air, and the water, alike refused shelter to a murderer.

THE LION · AND THE FOX.

A Fox entered into partnership with a Lion, on the
pretence of becoming his servant. Each undertook
his proper duty in accordance with his own nature
and powers. The Fox discovered and pointed out
the prey, the Lion sprung on it, and seized it. The
Fox soon became jealous of the Lion carrying off the
Lion's share, and said that he would no longer find
out the prey, but would capture it on his own account.
The next day he attempted to snatch a lamb from
the fold, but fell himself a prey to the huntsmen and
hounds.

THE LION AND THE EAGLE.

An Eagle stayed his flight, and entreated a Lion to make an alliance with him to their mutual advantage. The Lion replied, "I have no objection, but you must excuse me for requiring you to find surety for your good faith; for how can I trust any one as a friend, who is able to fly away from his bargain whenever he pleases?"

Try before you trust.

THE HEN AND THE SWALLOW.

A Hen finding the eggs of a viper, and carefully keeping them warm, nourished them into life. A Swallow observing what she had done, said, "You silly creature! why have you hatched these vipers, which, when they shall have grown, will inflict injury on all, beginning with yourself?"

THE FLEA AND THE WRESTLER.

A Flea settled upon the bare foot of a Wrestler, and bit him; on which he called loudly upon Hercules for help. The Flea a second time hopped upon his foot, when he groaned and said, "O Hercules! if you will not help me against a Flea, how can I hope for your assistance against greater antagonists?"

THE ASS AND HIS DRIVER.

An Ass being driven along the high road, suddenly started off, and bolted to the brink of a deep precipice. When he was in the act of throwing himself over, his owner, seizing him by the tail, endeavored to pull him back. The Ass, persisting in his effort, the man let him go and said, "Conquer: but conquer to your cost."

THE THRUSH AND THE FOWLER.

A Thrush was feeding on a myrtle-tree, and did not move from it, on account of the deliciousness of its berries. A Fowler observing her staying so long in one spot, having well birdlimed his reeds, caught

her. The Thrush, being at the point of death, exclaimed, "O foolish creature that I am! For the
sake of a little pleasant food I have deprived myself
of my life."

THE ROSE AND THE AMARANTH.

An Amaranth planted in a garden near a Rose-tree,
thus addressed it: "What a lovely flower is the Rose,
a favorite alike with Gods and with men. I envy
you your beauty and your perfume." The Rose replied, "I indeed, dear Amaranth, flourish but for a
brief season! If no cruel hand pluck me from my
stem, yet I must perish by an early doom. But thou
art *immortal*, and dost never fade, but bloomest for
ever in renewed youth."

THE TRAVELLERS AND THE PLANE-TREE.

Two Travellers, worn out by the heat of the summer's sun, laid themselves down at noon under the
wide-spreading branches of a Plane-tree. As they
rested under its shade, one of the Travellers said to
the other, "What a singularly useless tree is the
Plane! It bears no fruit, and is not of the least service to man." The Plane-tree, interrupting him,
said, "You ungrateful fellows! Do you, while re-
ceiving benefits from me, and resting under my
shade, dare to describe me as useless, and unprofit-
able?"

Some men despise their best blessings.

THE MOTHER
AND
THE WOLF.

A FAMISHED Wolf was prowling about in the morning in search of food. As he passed the door of a cottage built in the forest, he heard a Mother say to her child, "Be quiet, or I will throw you out of the window, and the Wolf shall eat you." The Wolf sat all day waiting at the door. In the evening he heard the same woman, fondling her child and saying: "He is quiet now, and if the Wolf should come, we will kill him." The Wolf, hearing these words, went home, gaping

with cold and hunger. On his reaching his den,
Mistress Wolf inquired of him why he returned
wearied and supperless, so contrary to his wont.
He replied: "Why, forsooth!—because I gave credence to the words of a woman!"

THE ASS AND THE HORSE.

An Ass besought a Horse to spare him a small portion of his feed. "Yes," said he; "if any remains
out of what I am now eating I will give it to you, for
the sake of my own superior dignity; and if you will
come when I shall reach my own stall in the evening, I will give you a little sack full of barley." The
Ass replied: "Thank you. I can't think that you,
who refuse me a little matter now, will by and by
confer on me a greater benefit."

THE CROW AND THE SHEEP.

A troublesome Crow seated herself on the back of
a Sheep. The Sheep, much against his will, carried
her backward and forward for a long time, and at
last said, "If you had treated a dog in this way, you
would have had your deserts from his sharp teeth."
To this the Crow replied, "I despise the weak, and
yield to the strong. I know whom I may bully, and
whom I must flatter; and I thus prolong my life to a
good old age."

THE PARTRIDGE AND THE FOWLER.

A FOWLER caught a Partridge, and was about to kill it. The Partridge earnestly besought him to spare his life, saying, "Pray, master, permit me to live, and I will entice many Partridges to you in recompense for your mercy to me." The Fowler replied, "I shall now with the less scruple take your life: because you are willing to save it at the cost of betraying your friends and relations."

THE FOX AND THE BRAMBLE.

A Fox, mounting a hedge, when he was about to fall caught hold of a Bramble. Having pricked and grievously torn the soles of his feet, he accused the Bramble, because, when he had fled to her for assistance, she had used him worse than the hedge itself. The Bramble, interrupting him, said, "But you really must have been out of your senses to fasten yourself on me, who am myself always accustomed to fasten upon others."

THE DOG AND THE OYSTER.

A Dog, used to eating eggs, saw an Oyster; and opening his mouth to its widest extent, swallowed it down with the utmost relish, supposing it to be an egg. Soon afterwards suffering great pain in his stomach, he said, "I deserve all this torment, for my folly in thinking that everything round must be an egg."

They who act without sufficient thought, will often fall into unsuspected danger.

THE FLEA AND THE MAN.

A Man, very much annoyed with a Flea, caught him at last, and said, "Who are you who dare to feed on my limbs, and to cost me so much trouble in catching you?" The Flea replied, "O my dear sir, pray spare my life, and destroy me not, for I cannot possibly do you much harm." The Man, laughing, replied, "Now you shall certainly die by mine own hands, for no evil, whether it be small or large, ought to be tolerated."

THE ASS AND THE CHARGER.

An Ass congratulated a Horse on being so ungrudgingly and carefully provided for, while he himself had scarcely enough to eat, nor even that without hard work. But when war broke out, and the heavy armed soldier mouted the Horse, and riding him to the charge, rushed into the very midst of the enemy, and the Horse, being wounded, fell dead on the battle-field; then the Ass, seeing all these things, changed his mind. and commiserated the Horse.

THE LION, JUPITER, AND THE ELEPHANT.

The Lion wearied Jupiter with his frequent complaints. "It is true," he said, "O Jupiter! that I am gigantic in strength, handsome in shape, and powerful in attack. I have jaws well provided with teeth, and feet furnished with claws, and I lord it over all the beasts of the forest; and what a disgrace it is, that being such as I am, I should be frightened by the crowing of a cock." Jupiter replied, "Why do you blame me without a cause? I have given you all the attributes which I possess myself, and your courage never fails you except in this one instance." On this the Lion groaned and lamented very much, and reproached himself with his cowardice, and wished that he might die. As these thoughts passed through his mind, he met an Elephant, and came near to hold a conversation with him. After a time he observed that the Elephant shook his ears very often, and he inquired what was the matter, and why his ears moved with such a tremor every now and then. Just at that moment a Gnat settled on the head of the Elephant, and he replied, "Do you see that little buzzing insect? If it enters my ear, my fate is sealed. I should die presently." The Lion said, "Well, since so huge a beast is afraid of a tiny gnat, I will no more complain, nor wish myself dead. I find myself, even as I am, better off than the Elephant, in that very same degree, that a Cock is greater than a Gnat."

THE LAMB AND THE WOLF.

A Wolf pursued a Lamb, which fled for refuge to a certain Temple. The Wolf called out to him and said, "The Priest will slay you in sacrifice, if he should catch you," on which the Lamb replied, "It would be better for me to be sacrificed in the Temple, than to be eaten by you,"

THE RICH MAN AND THE TANNER.

A RICH man lived near a Tanner, and not being able to bear the unpleasant smell of the tan-yard, he pressed his neighbor to go away. The Tanner put off his departure from time to time, saying that he would remove soon. But as he still continued to stay, it came to pass, as time went on, the rich man became accustomed to the smell, and feeling no manner of inconvenience, made no further complaints.

THE MULES AND THE ROBBERS.

Two MULES well laden with packs were trudging along. One carried panniers filled with money, the other sacks weighted with grain. The Mule carrying the treasure walked with head erect, as if conscious of the value of his burden, and tossed up and down the clear toned bells fastened to his neck. His companion followed with quiet and easy step. All on a sudden Robbers rushed from their hiding-places upon them, and in the scuffle with their owners, wounded with a sword the Mule carrying the treasure, which they greedily seized upon, while they took no notice of the grain. The Mule which had been robbed and wounded, bewailed his misfortunes. The other replied, "I am indeed glad that I was thought so little of, for I have lost nothing, nor am I hurt with any wound."

THE VIPER AND THE FILE.

A VIPER entering the workshop of a smith, sought from the tools the means of satisfying his hunger. He more particularly addressed himself to a File, and asked of him the favor of a meal. The File replied, "You must indeed be a simple-minded fellow if you expect to get anything from me, who am accustomed to take from every one, and never to give anything in return."

The covetous are poor givers,

THE LION AND THE SHEPHERD.

A LION, roaming through a forest, trod upon a thorn, and soon after came up towards a Shepherd, and fawned upon him, wagging his tail, as if he would say, "I am a suppliant, and seek your aid." The Shepherd boldly examined, and discovered the thorn, and placing his foot upon his lap, pulled it out and relieved the Lion of his pain, who returned into the forest. Some time after, the Shepherd being imprisoned on a false accusation, is condemned "to be cast to the Lions," as the punishment of his imputed crime. The Lion, on being released from his cage, recognizes the Shepherd as the man who healed him, and, instead of attacking him, approaches and places his foot upon his lap. The King, as soon as he heard the tale, ordered the Lion to be set free again in the forest, and the Shepherd to be pardoned and restored to his friends.

THE CAMEL AND JUPITER.

THE Camel, when he saw the Bull adorned with horns, envied him, and wished that he himself could obtain the same honors. He went to Jupiter, and besought him to give him horns. Jupiter, vexed at his request, because he was not satisfied with his size and strength of body, and desired yet more, not only refused to give him horns, but even deprived him of a portion of his ears,

THE PANTHER AND THE SHEPHERDS.

A Panther, by some mischance, fell into a pit. The Shepherds discovered him, and threw sticks at him, and pelted him with stones, while some of them, moved with compassion towards one about to die even though no one should hurt him, threw in some food to prolong his life. At night they returned home, not dreaming of any danger, but supposing that on the morrow they should find him dead. The Panther, however, when he had recruited his feeble strength, freed himself with a sudden bound from the pit, and hastened home with rapid steps to his den. After a few days he came forth and slaughtered the cattle, and, killing the Shepherds who had attacked him, raged with angry fury. Then they who had spared his life, fearing for their safety, surrendered to him their flocks, and begged only for their lives; to whom the Panther made this reply: " I remember alike those who sought my life with stones, and those who gave me food—lay aside, therefore, your fears. I return as an enemy only to those who injured me."

THE EAGLE AND THE KITE.

An Eagle, overwhelmed with sorrow, sat upon the branches of a tree, in company with a Kite. "Why," said the Kite, "do I see you with such a rueful look?" "I seek," she replied, "for a mate suitable for me, and am not able to find one." "Take me," returned the Kite, "I am much stronger than you are." "Why, are you able to secure the means of living by your plunder?" "Well, I have often caught and carried away an ostrich in my talons." The Eagle, persuaded by these words accepted him as her mate. Shortly after the nuptials the Eagle said, "Fly off, and bring me back the ostrich you promised me." The Kite, soaring aloft into the air, brought back the shabbiest possible mouse, and stinking from the length of time it had lain about the fields. "Is this," said the Eagle, "the faithful fulfilment of your promise to me?" The Kite replied, "That I might attain to your royal hand, there is nothing that I would not have promised, however much I knew that I must fail in the performance."

THE EAGLE AND HIS CAPTOR.

An Eagle was once captured by a man, who at once clipped his wings, and put him into his poultry yard with the other birds; at which treatment the Eagle was weighed down with grief. Another neighbor having purchased him, suffered his feathers to grow again. The Eagle took flight, and pouncing upon a hare brought it at once as an offering to his benefactor. A Fox, seeing this, exclaimed, "Do not propitiate the favor of this man, but of your former owner, lest he should again hunt for you, and deprive you a second time of your wings."

THE KING'S SON AND THE PAINTED LION.

A King who had one only son, fond of martial exercises, had a dream in which he was warned that his
son would be killed by a lion. Afraid lest the dream
should prove true, he built for his son a pleasant
palace, and adorned its walls for his amusement
with all kinds of animals of the size of life, among
which was the picture of a lion. When the young
Prince saw this, his grief at being thus confined
burst out afresh, and standing near the lion, he thus
spoke: "O you most detestable of animals! through
a lying dream of my father's, which he saw in his
sleep, I am shut up on your accourt in this palace as

if I had been a girl: what shall I now do to you?" With these words he stretched out his hands toward a thorn tree, meaning to cut a stick from its branches that he might beat the lion, when one of its sharp prickles pierced his finger, and caused great pain and inflammation, so that the young Prince fell down in a fainting fit. A violent fever suddenly set in, from which he died not many days after.

We had better bear our troubles bravely than try to escape them.

THE CAT AND VENUS.

A CAT fell in love with a handsome young man, and entreated Venus that she would change her into the form of a woman. Venus consented to her request, and transformed her into a beautiful damsel, so that the youth saw her, and loved her, and took her home as his bride. While they were reclining in their chamber, Venus, wishing to discover if the Cat in her change of shape had also altered her habits of life, let down a mouse in the middle of the room. She, quite forgetting her present condition, started up from the couch, and pursued the mouse, wishing to eat it. Venus, much disappointed, again caused her to return to her former shape.

Nature exceeds nurture.

THE EAGLE AND THE BEETLE.

The Eagle and the Beetle were at enmity together. and they destroyed one another's nests. The Eagle gave the first provocation in seizing upon, and in eating the young ones of the Beetle. The Beetle got by stealth at the Eagle's eggs, and rolled them out of the nest, and followed the Eagle even into the presence of Jupiter. On the Eagle making his complaint, Jupiter ordered him to make his nest in his lap; and while Jupiter had the eggs in his lap, the Beetle came flying about him, and Jupiter rising up unawares, to drive him away from his head, threw down the eggs, and broke them.

The weak often revenge themselves on those who use them ill, even though they be the more powerful.

THE SHE-GOATS AND THEIR BEARDS.

The She-goats having obtained by request from Jupiter the favor of a beard, the He-goats, sorely displeased, made complaint that the females equalled them in dignity. "Suffer them," said Jupiter, "to enjoy an empty honor, and to assume the badge of your noble sex, so long as they are not your equals in strength or courage."

It matters little if those who are inferior to us in merit should be like us in outside appearances.

THE BALD MAN AND THE FLY.

A Fly bit the bare head of a Bald Man, who endeavoring to destroy it, gave himself a heavy slap. Then said the Fly mockingly, "You who have wished to revenge, even with death, the prick of a tiny insect, what will you do to yourself, who have added insult to injury?" The Bald Man replied, "I can easily make peace with myself, because I know there was no intention to hurt. But you, an ill-favored and contemptible insect, who delight in sucking human blood, I wish that I could have killed you, even if I had incurred a heavier penalty."

THE SHIPWRECKED MAN AND THE SEA.

A Shipwrecked Man, having been cast upon a certain shore, slept after his buffetings with the deep. After a while waking up, when he looked upon the sea, he loaded it with reproaches that, enticing men with the calmness of its looks, when it had induced them to plough its waters, it grew rough and destroyed them utterly. The Sea, assuming the form of a woman, replied to him: "Blame not me, my good sir, but the winds, for I am by my own nature as calm and firm even as this earth; but the winds falling on me on a sudden, create these waves, and lash me into fury."

THE BUFFOON AND THE COUNTRYMAN.

A RICH nobleman once opened the theatres without
charge to the people, and gave a public notice that
he would handsomely reward any person who should
invent a new amusement for the occasion.   Various
public performers contended for the prize.   Among
them came a Buffoon well known among the popu-
lace for his jokes, and said that he had a kind of
entertainment which had never been brought out on
any stage before.   This report being spread about
made a great stir in the place, and the theatre was
crowded in every part.   The Buffoon appeared alone
upon the boards, without any apparatus or confed-

erates, and the very sense of expectation caused an intense silence. The Buffoon suddenly bent his head towards his bosom, and imitated the squeaking of a little pig so admirably with his voice, that the audience declared that he had a porker under his cloak, and demanded that it should be shaken out. When that was done, and yet nothing was found, they cheered the actor, and loaded him with the loudest applause. A Countryman in the crowd, observing all that had passed, said, "So help me, Hercules, he shall not beat me at that trick!" and at once proclaimed that he would do the same thing on the next day, though in a much more natural way. On the morrow a still larger crowd assembled in the theatre; but now partiality for their favorite actor very generally prevailed, and the audience came rather to ridicule the Countryman than to see the spectacle. Both of the performers, however, appeared on the stage. The Buffoon grunted and squeaked very fast, and obtained, as on the preceding day, the applause and cheers of the spectators. Next the Countryman commenced, and pretending that he concealed a little pig beneath his clothes (which in truth he did, but not suspected of the audience) contrived to lay hold of and to pull his ear, when he began to squeak, and to express in his pain the actual cry of the pig. The crowd, however, cried out with one consent that the Buffoon had given a far more exact imitation, and clamored for the Countryman to be kicked out of the theatre. On this the rustic produced the little pig from his cloak, and showed by the most positive proof the greatness of their mistake. "Look here," he said, "this shows what sort of judges you are."

THE CROW AND THE SERPENT.

A Crow, in great want of food, saw a Serpent asleep in a sunny nook, and flying down, greedily seized him. The Serpent turning about, bit the Crow with a mortal wound; the Crow in the agony of death exclaimed. "O unhappy me! who have found in that which I deemed a happy windfall the source of my destruction."

THE HUNTER AND THE HORSEMAN.

A certain Hunter having snared a hare, placed it upon his shoulders, and set out homewards. He met on his way with a man on horseback who begged the hare of him, under the pretence of purchasing it. The Horseman having got the hare, rode off as fast as he could. The Hunter ran after him, as if he was sure of overtaking him. The Horseman, however, increasing more and more the distance between them, the Hunter, sorely against his will, called out to him, and said. "Get along with you! for I will now make you a present of the hare."

THE OLIVE-TREE AND THE FIG-TREE.

THE Olive-tree ridiculed the Fig-tree because, while she was green all the year round, the Fig-tree changed its leaves with the seasons. A shower of snow fell upon them, and, finding the Olive full of foliage, it settled upon its branches, and, breaking them down with its weight, at once despoiled it of its beauty and killed the tree; but finding the Fig-tree denuded of leaves, it fell through to the ground, and did not injure it at all.

THE FROGS' COMPLAINT AGAINST THE SUN.

ONCE upon a time, when the Sun announced his intention to take a wife, the Frogs lifted up their voices in clamor to the sky. Jupiter, disturbed by the noise of their croaking, inquired the cause of their complaint. One of them said, "The Sun, now while he is single, parches up the marsh, and compels us to die miserably in our arid homes; what will be our future condition if he should beget other suns?"

THE MOUSE, THE FROG, AND THE HAWK.

A MOUSE who always lived on the land, by an unlucky chance formed an intimate acquaintance with a Frog, who lived for the most part in the water. The Frog, one day intent on mischief, bound the foot of the Mouse tightly to his own. Thus joined together, the Frog first of all led his friend the Mouse to the meadow where they were accustomed to find their food. After this, he gradually led him toward the pool in which he lived, until he reached the very brink, when suddenly jumping in he dragged the Mouse in with him. The Frog enjoyed the water amazingly, and swam croaking about, as if he had done a meritorious action. The unhappy Mouse was soon suffocated with the water, and his dead body floated about on the surface, tied to the foot of the Frog. A Hawk observed it, and, pouncing upon it with his talons, carried it up aloft. The Frog being still fastened to the leg of the Mouse, was also carried off a prisoner, and was eaten by the Hawk.

Harm hatch, harm catch.

THE ÆTHIOP.

THE purchaser of a black servant was persuaded that the color of his skin arose from dirt contracted through the neglect of his former masters. On bringing him home he resorted to every means of cleaning, and subjected him to incessant scrubbings. He caught a severe cold, but he never changed his color or complexion.

What's bred in the bone will stick to the flesh.

THE FISHERMAN AND HIS NETS.

A FISHERMAN, engaged in his calling, made a very successful cast, and captured a great haul of fish. He managed by a skilful handling of his net to retain all the large fish, and to draw them to the shore; but he could not prevent the smaller fish from falling back through the meshes of the net into the sea.

THE LION AND THE FOUR BULLS.

Four Bulls, which had entered into a very strict friendship, kept always near one another, and fed together. The Lion often saw them, and as often had a mind to make one of them his prey ; but, though he could have subdued any of them singly, yet he was afraid to attack the whole alliance, as knowing they would have been too strong for him, and therefore he contented himself, for the present, with keeping at a distance. At last, perceiving no attempt was to be made upon them as long as this combination held, he took occasion, by whispers and hints, to foment jealousies, and raise divisions among them: This stratagem succeeded so well, that the Bulls grew cold and reserved towards one another, which soon after ripened into a downright hatred and aversion ; and, at last, ended in a total separation. The Lion had now obtained his ends ; and, as impossible as it was for him to hurt them while they were united, he found no difficulty, now they were parted, to seize and devour every Bull of them, one after another.

"United we stand ; divided we fall."

THE ASS EATING THISTLES.

An Ass was loaded with good provisions of several sorts, which, in time of harvest, he was carrying into the field for his master and the reapers to dine upon. By the way he met with a fine large Thistle, and, being very hungry, began to mumble it ; which, while he was doing, he entered into this reflection —"How many greedy epicures would think themselves happy, amidst such a variety of delicate viands as I now carry! But to me, this bitter, prickly Thistle is more savory and relishing than the most exquisite and sumptuous banquet."

Every to his taste: one man's meat is another man's poison, and one man's poison is another man's meat.

THE COCK AND THE FOX.

THE Fox, passing early one summer's morning near a farm-yard, was caught in a springe, which the farmer had planted there for that end. The Cock, at a distance, saw what happened, and, hardly yet daring to trust himself too near so dangerous a foe, approached him cautiously, and peeped at him, not without some horror and dread of mind. Reynard no sooner perceived it, but he addressed himself to him, with all the designing artifice imaginable. "Dear cousin," says he, "you see what an unfortunate accident has befallen me here, and all upon your account: for, as I was creeping through yonder hedge, in my way homeward, I heard you crow, and was resolved to ask you how you did before I went any further; but, by the way, I met with this disaster; and therefore now I must become an humble suitor to you for a knife to cut this plaguy string; or, at least, that you would conceal my misfortune, till I have knawed it asunder with my teeth." The Cock, seeing how the case stood, made no reply, but posted away as fast as he could, and gave the farm-

er an account of the whole matter; who, taking a
good weapon along with him, came and did the
Fox's business, before he could have time to contrive
his escape.

It is the duty of humanity to succor the unfortunate and the troubled; but to aid the vicious and the
evil-minded is to become a partner in their guilt.

THE FROG AND THE FOX.

A FROG, leaping out of the lake, and taking the
advantage of a rising ground, made proclamation to
all the beasts of the forest, that he was an able physician, and, for curing all manner of distempers,
would turn his back to no person living. This dis-
course, uttered in a parcel of hard, cramped words,
which nobody understood, made the beasts admire
his learning, and give credit to everything he said.
At last the Fox, who was present, with indignation
asked him, how he could have the impudence, with
those thin lantern-jaws, that meagre, pale phiz, and
blotched, spotted body, to set up for one who was
able to cure the infirmities of others.

" Physician heal thyself."

THE FOX IN THE WELL.

A Fox, having fallen into a Well, made a shift, by
sticking his claws into the sides, to keep his head
above water. Soon after, a Wolf came and peeped

over the brink ; to whom the Fox applied himself very earnestly for assistance ; entreating that he would help him to a rope, or something of that kind, which might favor his escape. The Wolf, moved with compassion at his misfortune, could not forbear expressing his concern ; ".Ah ! poor Reynard," says he, "I am sorry for you with all my heart ; how could you possibly come into this melancholy condition ?" "Nay, prithee, friend," replies the Fox, "if you wish me well, do not stand pitying of me, but lend me some succor as fast as you can : for pity is but cold comfort when one is up to the chin in water, and within a hair's breadth of starving or drowning."

A grain of help is worth a bushel of pity.

THE FOWLER AND THE RINGDOVE.

A FOWLER took his gun, and went into the woods a shooting. He spied a Ringdove among the branches of an oak, and intended to kill it. He clapped the piece to his shoulder, and took his aim accordingly. But, just as he was going to pull the trigger, an adder, which he had trod upon under the grass, stung him so painfully in the leg, that he was forced to quit his design, and threw his gun down in a passion. The poison immediately infected his blood, and his whole body began to mortify ; which, when he perceived, he could not help owning it to be just. "Fate," says he, "has brought destruction upon me while I was contriving the death of another."

There is a law of retribution governing life. Men often fall into the very pit they dig for others.

THE TUNNY AND THE DOLPHIN.

A FISH called a Tunny, being pursued by a Dolphin, and driven with great violence, not minding which way he went, was thrown by the force of the waves upon a rock, and left there. His death now was inevitable; but, casting his eyes on one side, and seeing the Dolphin in the same condition lie gasping by him — "Well," says he, "I must die, it is true; but I die with pleasure, when I behold him who is the cause of it involved in the same fate."

Revenge is sweet, even in death.

THE BOAR AND THE ASS.

A LITTLE scoundrel of an Ass, happening to meet with a Boar, had a mind to be arch upon him: "And so, brother," says he, "your humble servant." The Boar, somewhat nettled at his familiarity, bristled up to him, and told him he was surprised to hear him utter so impudent an untruth, and was just going to show his noble resentment by giving him a rip in the flank; but wisely stifling his passion, he contented himself with only saying—"Go, you sorry beast! I could be amply and easily revenged of you, but I do not care to foul my tusks with the blood of so base a creature."

Dignity cannot afford to quarrel with its inferiors.

THE HORSE AND THE LOADED ASS.

An idle Horse, and an Ass laboring under a heavy **burden**, were travelling the road· together; they both belonged to a country fellow, who trudged it on foot by them. The Ass, ready to faint under his heavy load, entreated the **Horse** to assist him, and lighten his burden, by taking some of it upon his back. The Horse was ill-natured and refused to do it; upon which the poor Ass tumbled down in the midst of the highway, and expired in an instant. The countryman ungirded his pack-saddle, and tried several ways to relieve him, but all to no purpose; which, when he perceived, he took the whole burden, and laid it upon the Horse, together with the skin of the dead Ass; so that the Horse, by his moroseness in refusing to do a small kindness, justly brought upon himself a great inconvenience.

Selfishness often prepares a burden as well as a rod for its own back.

THE PEACOCK AND THE MAGPIE.

The birds met together upon a time to choose a king; and the Peacock standing candidate, displayed his gaudy plumes, and caught the eyes of the silly multitude with the richness of his feathers. The majority declared for him, and clapped their wings with great applause; but, just as they were going to proclaim him, the Magpie stepped forth in the midst of the assembly, and addressed himself thus to the new king "May it please your majesty elect to permit one of your unworthy subjects to represent to you his suspicions and apprehensions, in the face of this whole congregation, we have chosen you for our king, we have put our lives and fortunes into your hands, and our whole hope and dependence is upon you; if therefore the eagle, or the vulture, or the kite, should at any time make a descent upon us, as it is highly probable they will, may your majesty be so gracious as to dispel our fears, and clear our doubts about that matter, by letting us know how you intend to defend us against them?" This pithy unanswerable question drew the whole audience into so just a reflection, that they soon resolved to proceed to a new choice. But, from that time, the Peacock has been looked upon as a vain, insignificant pretender, and the Magpie esteemed as eminent as a speaker as any among the whole community of birds.

A king chosen for his adornments, will bring his people to shame.

THE KITE AND THE PIGEONS.

A KITE, who had kept sailing in the air for many days near a dove-house, and made a stoop at several Pigeons, but all to no purpose, (for they were too nimble for him,) at last had recourse to stratagem, and took his opportunity one day to make a declaration to them, in which he set forth his own just and good intentions, who had nothing more at heart than the defence and protection of the Pigeons in their ancient rights and liberties, and how concerned he was at their fears and jealousies of a foreign invasion, especially their unjust and unreasonable suspicions of himself, as if he intended, by force of arms, to break in upon their constitution, and erect a tyrannical government over them. To prevent all which, and thoroughly quiet their minds, he thought proper to propose to them such terms of alliance and articles of peace as might forever cement a good understanding between them ; the principal of which was, that they should accept of him for their king, and invest him with all kingly privilege and prerogative over them. The poor simple Pigeons consented ; the Kite took the coronation oath after a very solemn manner, on his part, and the Doves, the oaths of allegiance and fidelity, on theirs. But much time had not passed over their heads, before the good Kite pretended that it was part of his prerogative to devour a Pigeon whenever he pleased. And this he was not contented to do himself only, but instructed the rest of the royal family in the same kingly arts of government. The Pigeons, reduced to this miserable condition, said one to the other, "Ah! we deserve no better! Why did we let him come in?"

Men should look before they leap. A too ready loyalty often leads to peril.

THE SWALLOW AND OTHER BIRDS.

A Farmer was sowing his field with flax. The Swallow observed it, and desired the other Birds to assist her in picking the seed up and destroying it, telling them that flax was that pernicious material of which the thread was composed which made the fowler's nets, and by that means contributed to the ruin of so many innocent Birds. But the poor Swallow not having the good fortune to be regarded, the flax sprung up, and appeared above the ground. She then put them in mind once more of their impending danger, and wished them to pluck it up in the bud before it went any farther. They still neglected her warnings, and the flax grew up into the high stalk. She yet again desired them to attack it, for that it was not yet too late. But all that she could get was to be ridiculed and despised for a silly, pretending prophet. The Swallow finding all her remonstrances availed nothing, was resolved to leave the society of such unthinking, careless creatures, before it was too late. So quitting the woods, she repaired to the houses, and forsaking the conversation of the Birds, has ever since made her abode among the dwellings of men.

When people in peril will not heed good advice, they must bear the entire responsibility of their foolish conduct.

THE WANTON CALF.

A CALF, full of play and wantonness, seeing the Ox at plough, could not forbear insulting him. "What a sorry poor drudge art thou," says he, "to bear that heavy yoke upon your neck, and go all day drawing a plow at your tail, to turn up the ground for your master! but you are a wretched dull slave,

and know no better, or else you would not do it. See
what a happy life I lead : I go just where I please ;
sometimes I lie down under the cool shade ; sometimes frisk about in the open sunshine ; and, when
I please, slake my thirst in the clear sweet brook ;
but you, if you were to perish, have not so much as
a little dirty water to refresh you." The Ox, not at
all moved with what he said, went quietly and calmly on with his work ; and, in the evening was un-
yoked and turned loose. Soon after which he saw
the calf taken out of the field, and delivered into the
hands of a priest, who immediately led him to the
altar, and prepared to sacrifice him. His head was
hung round with fillets of flowers, and the fatal
knife was just going to be applied to his throat,
when the Ox drew near and whispered him to this
purpose : "Behold the end of your insolence and
arrogance ; it was for this only you were suffered to
live at all ; and pray now, friend, whose condition is
best, yours or mine?"

Boastful idleness often comes to grief.

THE HUSBANDMAN AND THE STORK.

THE Husbandman pitched a net in his fields to take
the cranes and geese which came to feed upon the
new-sown corn. Accordingly he took several, both
cranes and geese ; and among them a Stork, who
pleaded hard for his life, and, among other apologies which he made, alleged, that he was neither
goose nor crane, but a poor harmless Stork, who
performed his duty to his parents to all intents and
purposes, feeding them when they were old, and, as

occasion required, carrying them from place to place upon his back. "All this may be true," replied the Husbandman ; "but, as I have taken you in bad company, and in the same crime, you must expect to suffer the same punishment."

However good a man may be he cannot afford to mix with evil companions.

THE HORSE AND THE LION.

A Lion seeing a fine plump Nag, had a great mind to eat a bit of him, but knew not which way to get him into his power. At last he bethought himself of this contrivance ; he gave out that he was a physician, who, having gained experience by his travels into foreign countries, had made himself capable of curing any sort of malady or distemper incident to any kind of beast, hoping by this stratagem to get an easier admittance among cattle, and find an opportunity to execute his design. The Horse, who smoked the matter, was resolved to be even with him ; and, so humoring the thing as if he suspected nothing, he prayed the Lion to give him his advice in relation to a thorn he had got in his foot, which had quite lamed him, and gave him great pain and uneasiness. The Lion readily agreed, and desired he might see the foot. Upon which the Horse lifted up one of his hind legs, and, while the Lion pretended to be poring earnestly upon his hoof, gave him such a kick in the face as quite stunned him, and left him sprawling upon the ground. In the mean time the Horse trotted away, neighing and laughing merrily at the success of the trick, by which he

had defeated the purpose of one who intended to
have tricked him out of his life.

The sharpest tricksters are often overmatched.
The engineer gets "hoist with his own petard."

CUPID AND DEATH.

CUPID, one sultry summer's noon, tired with play,
and faint with heat, went into a cool grotto to repose
himself, which happened to be the cave of Death.
He threw himself carelessly down on the floor, and
his quiver turning topsy-turvy, all the arrows fell
out, and mingled with those of Death, which lay
scattered up and down the place. When he awoke
he gathered them up as well as he could, but they
were so intermingled that, though he knew the certain number, he could not rightly distinguish them;
from which it happened that he took up some of the
arrows which belonged to Death, and left several of
his own in the room of them. This is the cause that
we, now and then, see the hearts of the old and de-
crepit transfixed with the bolts of love; and with
equal grief and surprise behold the youthful bloom-
ing part of our species smitten with the darts of
Death.

Cupid's arrows are as perilous as they are capri-
cious.

THE OLD MAN AND HIS SONS.

AN Old Man had many Sons, who were often falling
out with one another. When the Father had exert-
ed his authority, and used other means in order to

reconcile them, and all to no purpose, at last he had recourse to this expedient; he ordered his Sons to be called before him, and a short bundle of sticks to be brought; and then commanded them, one by one, to try if, with all their might and strength, they could any of them break it. They all tried, but to no purpose; for the sticks being closely and compactly bound up together, it was impossible for the force of man to do it. After this the Father ordered the bundle to be untied, and gave a single stick to each of his Sons; at the same time bidding him try to break it : which, when each did with all imaginable ease, the Father addressed himself to to them to this effect,—"O my Sons, behold the power of unity! For if you, in like manner, would but keep yourselves strictly conjoined in the bonds of friendship, it would not be in the power of any mortal to hurt you; but, when once the ties of brotherly affection are dissolved, how soon do you fall to pieces, and are liable to be violated by every injurious hand that assaults you!"

Unity is strength.

THE STAG AND THE FAWN.

A Stag, grown old and mischievous, was, according to custom, stamping with his foot, making offers with his head, and bellowing so terribly, that the whole herd quaked for fear of him; when one of the little Fawns coming up, addressed him to this purpose, — "Pray, what is the reason that you, who are so stout and formidable at all other times, if you do but hear the cry of the hounds are ready to fly out of your skin for fear ?"— "What you observe is true," replied the Stag, "though I know not how to account for it : I am indeed vigorous, and able enough, I think, to make my party good anywhere, and often resolve with myself that nothing shall ever dismay my courage for the future ; but, alas! I no sooner hear the voice of a hound but my spirits fail me, and I cannot help making off as fast as ever my legs can carry me."

The greatest braggarts are generally the most abject cowards.

THE HAWK AND THE FARMER.

A Hawk, pursuing a pigeon over a corn field with great eagerness and force, threw himself into a net which a husbandman had planted there to take the crows ; who being employed not far off, and seeing the Hawk fluttering in the net, came and took him; but, just as he was going to kill him, the Hawk besought him to let him go, assuring him that he was only following a pigeon, and neither intended nor had done any harm to him. To whom the Farmer replied, "And what harm had the poor pigeon done to you ?" Upon which he wrung his head off immediately.

Oppressors are never short of excuses for their evil designs.

THE NURSE AND THE WOLF.

A Nurse, who was endeavoring to quiet a froward, bawling child, among other attempts, threatened to throw it out of doors to the Wolf, if it did not leave off crying. A Wolf, who chanced to be prowling near the door just at that time, heard the expression, and, believing the woman to be in earnest, waited a long while about the house in expectation of seeing her words made good. But at last the child, wearied with its own importunities, fell asleep, and the poor Wolf was forced to return back to the woods empty and supperless. The fox meeting him, and surprised to see him going home so thin and disconsolate, asked him what the matter was, and how he came to speed no better that night; "Ah! do not ask me," says he; "I was so silly as to believe what the Nurse said, and have been disappointed."

Even Wolves are sometimes too trustful

THE SATYR AND TRAVELER.

A Satyr, as he was ranging the forest in an exceeding cold, snowy season, met with a Traveler half-starved with the extremity of the weather. He took compassion on him, and kindly invited him home to a warm comfortable cave he had in the hollow of a rock. As soon as they entered and sat down, notwithstanding there was a good fire in the place, the chilly Traveler could not forbear blowing his fingers' ends. Upon the Satyr's asking him why he did so, he answered, that he did it to warm his hands. The honest sylvan having seen little of the world, admired a man who was master of so valuable a quality as that of blowing heat, and therefore was resolved to entertain him in the best manner he could,

He spread the table before him with dried fruits of several sorts; and produced a remnant of cold cordial wine, which, as the rigor of the season made very proper, he mulled with some warm spices, infused over the fire, and presented to his shivering guest. But this the traveler thought to blow likewise; and upon the Satyr's demanding a reason why he blowed again, he replied, to cool his dish. This second answer provoked the Satyr's indignation as much as the first had kindled his surprise: so, taking the man by the shoulder, he thrust him out of doors, saying, he would have nothing to do with a wretch who had so vile a quality as to blow hot and cold with the same mouth.

The meanest of men is he who combines in himself the flatterer and the slanderer.

THE ENVIOUS MAN AND THE COVETOUS.

An Envious Man happened to be offering up his prayers to Jupiter just in the time and place with a covetous miserable fellow. Jupiter, not caring to be troubled with their impertinences himself, sent Apollo to examine the merits of their petitions, and to give them such relief as he should think proper. Apollo therefore opened his commission, and withal told them that, to make short of the matter, whatever the one asked the other should have it double. Upon this, the Covetous Man, though he had a thousand things to request, yet forbore to ask first, hoping to receive a double quantity; for he concluded that all men's wishes sympathized with his. By this means the Envious Man had an opportunity of preferring his petition first, which was the thing he aimed at ; so, without much hesitation, he prayed to be relieved, by having one of his eyes put out: knowing that, of consequence, his companion would be deprived of both.

Envy and Avarice are twin brothers of an evil house, as cruel as they are selfish.

THE TWO POTS.

An Earthen Pot, and one of Brass, standing together upon the river's brink, were both carried away by the flowing in of the tide. The Earthen Pot showed some uneasiness, as fearing he should be broken; but his companion of Brass bid him be under no apprehensions, for that he would take care of him. "O," replies the other, "keep as far off as ever you can, I entreat you ; it is you I am most afraid of : for, whether the stream dashes you against me, or me against you, I am sure to be the sufferer; and, therefore, I beg of you, do not let us come near one another."

We are often in greatest peril from well intending friends.

THE FOX AND THE STORK.

The Fox invited the Stork to dinner, and, being disposed to divert himself at the expense of his guest, provided nothing for the entertainment but a soup, in a wide, shallow dish. This himself could lap up with a great deal of ease ; but the Stork, who could but just dip in the point of his bill, was not a bit better all the while : however, in a few days after, he returned the compliment, and invited the Fox ; but suffered nothing to be brought to the table but some minced meat in a glass jar, the neck of which was so deep and so narrow, that, though the Stork with his long bill made a shift to fill his belly, all that the Fox, who was very hungy, could do, was to lick the brims, as the Stork slabbered them with his eating. Reynard was heartily vexed at first, but, when he came to take his leave, owned ingenuously, that he had been used as he deserved, and that he had no reason to take any threatment ill, of which himself had set the example.

The Fox may be full of cunning but the Stork is a match for him.

THE BEAR AND THE BEE-HIVES.

A Bear, climbing over the fence into a place where Bees were kept, began to plunder the Hives, and rob them of their honey. But the Bees, to revenge the injury, attacked him in a whole swarm together ; and, though they were not able to pierce his rugged hide, yet, with their little stings, they so annoyed his eyes and nostrils, that, unable to endure the smarting pain, with impatience he tore the skin over his ears with his own claws, and suffered ample punishment for the injury he did the Bees in breaking open their waxen cells.

Ill-gotten gains bring many pains,

THE EAGLE AND THE CROW.

An Eagle flew down from the top of a high rock, and settled upon the back of a lamb ; and then instantly flying up into the air again, bore his bleating prize aloft in his pounces. A Crow who sat upon an elm, and beheld the exploit, resolved to imitate it ; so flying down upon the back of a ram, and entangling his claws in the wool, he fell a chattering and attempting to fly ; by which means he drew the observation of the shepherd upon him, who finding his feet hampered in the fleece of the ram, easily took him, and gave him to his boys for their sport and diversion.

It is not always safe to imitate a bad example.

THE DOG AND THE SHEEP.

The Dog sued the Sheep for debt, of which the kite and the wolf were to be judges. They, without debating long upon the matter. or making any scruple for want of evidence, gave sentence for the plaintiff; who immediately tore the poor Sheep in pieces, and divided the spoil with the unjust judges.

Justice can only be obtained by an appeal to righteous judges.

THE YOUNG MAN AND THE SWALLOW.

A prodigal young spendthrift, who had wasted his whole patrimony in taverns and gaming-houses, among lewd, idle company, was taking a melancholy walk near a brook. It was in the month of January; and happened to be one of those warm sunshiny days which sometimes smile upon us even in that winterly season of the year ; and to make it the more flattering, a Swallow, which had made his appearance, by mistake, too soon, flew skimming along upon the surface of the water. The giddy Youth observing this, without any farther consideration, concluded that summer was now come, and that he should have little or no occasion for clothes, so he went and pawned them at the broker's, and ventured the money for one stake more, among his sharping companions. When this too was gone the same way with the rest, he took another solitary walk in the same place as before. But the weather being severe and frosty, had made everything look with an aspect very different from what it did before ; the brook was quite frozen over, and the poor Swallow lay dead upon the bank of it; the very sight of which cooled the young Spark's brains; and coming to a sense of his misery, he reproached the deceased bird as the author of all his misfortunes:— " Ah, wretch that thou wert !" says he, " thou hast undone both thyself and me, who was so credulous as to depend upon thee."

The spendthrift blames everybody but himself for his poverty.

THE WOOD AND THE CLOWN.

A Country Fellow came one day into the wood, and looked about him with some concern ; upon

which the Trees, with a curiosity natural to some
other creatures, asked him what he wanted. He re-
replied, "That he only wanted a piece of wood to
make a handle to his hatchet." Since that was all,
it was voted unanimously that he should have a
piece of good, sound, tough ash. But he no sooner
received and fitted it for his purpose, than he began
to lay about him unmercifully, and to hack and hew
without distinction, felling the noblest trees in all
the forest. Then the Oak is said to have spoke thus to
the Beech in a low whisper, — "Brother, we must
take it for our pains."

Beware of small concessions.

THE FOX AND THE TIGER.

A SKILLFUL archer coming into the woods, directed
his arrows so successfully, that he slew many wild
beasts, and pursued several others. This put the
whole savage kind into a fearful consternation, and
made them fly to the most retired thickets for
refuge. At last, the Tiger resumed a courage, and,
bidding them not be afraid, said, that he alone would
engage the enemy; telling them, they might depend
upon his valor and strength to revenge their wrongs.
In the midst of these threats, while he was lashing
himself with his tail, and tearing up the ground for
anger, an arrow pierced his ribs, and hung by its
barbed point in his side. He set up an hideous and
loud roar, occasioned by the anguish which he felt,
and endeavored to draw out the painful dart with
his teeth; when the Fox, approaching him, inquired
with an air of surprise, who it was that could have

strength and courage enough to wound so mighty and valorous a beast! "Ah!" says the Tiger, "I was mistaken in my reckoning : it was that invincible man yonder."

It is never wise to be to boastful. There is always some vulnerable point in the strongest armor.

JUPITER AND THE CAMEL.

The Camel presented a petition to Jupiter, complaining of the hardship of his case in not having, like bulls and other creatures, horns, or any weapons of defence, to protect himself from the attacks of his enemies, and praying that relief might be given him in such manner as might be thought most expedient, Jupiter could not help smiling at the impertinent address of the great silly beast, but, however, rejected the petition; and told him that, so far from granting his unreasonable request, henceforward he would take care his ears should be shortened, as a punishment for his presumptuous importunity.

Dissatisfaction tends to diminish the value of present possessions.

THE WIND AND THE SUN.

A dispute once arose betwixt the north Wind and the Sun, about the superiority of their power ; and they agreed to try their strength upon a traveler, which should be able to get his cloak off first. The north Wind began, and blew a very cold blast, accompanied with a sharp driving shower. But this, and whatever else he could do, instead of making the man quit his cloak, obliged him to gird it about his body as close as possible. Next came the Sun; who, breaking out from a thick watery cloud, drove away the cold vapors for the sky, and darted his warm sultry rays upon the head of the poor weather-beaten traveler. The man growing faint with the heat, and unable to endure it any longer, first throws off his heavy cloak, and then flies for protection to the shade of a neighboring grove.

Extremes are always dangerous; a medium course is always most to be desired.

THE OLD WOMAN AND HER MAIDS.

A CERTAIN Old Woman had several Maids, whom she used to call up to their work, every morning, at the crowing of the cock. The Wenches, who found it grievous to have their sweet sleep disturbed so early, combined together, and killed the cock; thinking that, when the alarm was gone, they might enjoy themselves in their warm beds a little longer. The Old Woman, grieved for the loss of her cock, and having, by some means or other, discovered the whole plot, was resolved to be even with them; for, from that time, she obliged them to rise constantly at midnight.

In rash endeavors to reduce existing ills, we may easily increase our troubles.

THE PORCUPINE AND THE SNAKES.

A Porcupine, wanting to shelter himself, desired a nest of Snakes to give him admittance into their cave. They were prevailed upon, and let him in accordingly; but were so annoyed with his sharp prickly quills that they soon repented of their easy compliance, and entreated the Porcupine to withdraw, and leave them their hole to themselves. "No," says he, "let them quit the place that don't like it; for my part, I am well enough satisfied as I am."

Hospitality is a virtue but should be wisely exercised, we may by thoughtlessness entertain foes instead of friends.

THE CAT AND THE FOX.

As the Cat and the Fox were talking politics together on a time, in the middle of a forest, Reynard said, "Let things turn out ever so bad, he did not care, for he had a thousand tricks for them yet, before they should hurt him." "But pray," says he, "Mrs. Puss, suppose there should be an invasion, what course do you design to take?" "Nay," says the Cat, "I have but one shift for it, and if that won't do, I am undone." "I am sorry for you," replies Reynard, "with all my heart, and would gladly furnish you with one or two of mine, but indeed, neighbor, as times go, it is not good to trust; we must even be every one for himself, as the saying is, and so your humble servant." These words were scarcely out of his mouth, when they were alarmed with a pack of hounds, that came upon them full cry. The Cat, by the help of her single shift, ran up a tree, and sat securely among the top branches; from whence she beheld Reynard, who had not been able to get out of sight, overtaken with his thousand tricks, and torn in as many pieces by the dogs which had surrounded him.

A little common sense is often of more value than much cunning.

THE LION AND OTHER BEASTS.

THE Lion and several other beasts entered into an alliance offensive and defensive, and were to live very sociably together in the forest. One day, having made a sort of an excursion by way of hunting, they took a very fine, large, fat deer, which was divided into four parts ; there happening to be then present his majesty the Lion, and only three others. After the division was made, and the parts were set out, his majesty, advancing forward some steps and pointing to one of the shares, was pleased to declare himself after the following manner : "This I seize and take possesion of as my right, which devolves to me, as I am descended by a true, lineal, hereditary succession from the royal family of Lion : that (pointing to the second) I claim by, I think, no unreasonable demand; considering that all the engagements you have with the enemy turn chiefly upon my courage and conduct; and you very well know, that wars are too expensive to be carried on without proper supplies. Then (nodding his head towards the third) that I shall take by virtue of my prerogative; to which, I make no question, but so dutiful and loyal a people will pay all the deference and regard that I can desire. Now, as for the remaining part, the necessity of our present affairs is so very urgent, our stock so low, and our credit so impaired and weakened, that I must insist upon your granting that, without any hesitation or demur; and hereof fail not at your peril."

We should be careful how we place ourselves at the mercy of the powerful.

THE FATAL MARRIAGE.

THE Lion touched with gratitude by the noble procedure of a Mouse, and resolving not to be outdone in generosity by any wild beast whatsoever, desired his little deliverer to name his own terms, for that he might depend upon his complying with any proposal he should make. The Mouse, fired with ambition at this gracious offer, did not so much consider what was proper for him to ask, as what was in the power of his prince to grant; and so presumptuously demanded his princely daughter, the young Lioness, in marriage. The Lion consented; but, when he would have given the royal virgin into his possession, she, like a giddy thing as she was, not minding how she walked, by chance set her paw upon her spouse, who was coming to meet her, and crushed her little dear to pieces.

Ambition oftentimes overleaps itself and falls into great peril.

THE ANT AND THE FLY.

ONE day there happened some words between the Ant and the Fly about precedency, and the point was argued with great warmth and eagerness on both sides. Says the Fly, " It is well known what my pretensions are, and how justly they are grounded : there is never a sacrifice offered but I always taste of the entrails, even before the gods themselves. I have one of the uppermost seats at church, and frequent the altar as often as anybody : I have a free admission at court ; and can never want the king's ear, for I sometimes sit upon his shoulder. There is not a maid of honor, or handsome young creature comes in my way, but, if I like her, I settle betwixt her balmy lips. And then I eat and drink the best of everything, without having any occasion to work for my living. What is there that such country pusses as you enjoy to be compared to a life like this ? " The Ant, who by this time had composed herself, replied with a great deal of temper, and no less severity—" Indeed, to be a guest at an entertainment of the gods is a very great honor, if one is invited; but I should not care to be a disagreeable intruder anywhere. You talk of the king and the court, and the fine ladies there, with great familiarity; but, as I have been getting in my harvest in summer, I have seen a certain person under the town walls making a hearty meal upon something that is not so proper to be mentioned. As to your frequenting the altars, you are in the right to take sanctuary where you are like to meet with the least disturbance; but I have known people before now run to altars, and call it devotion, when they have been shut out of all good company, and had nowhere else to go. You do not work for your living, you say—true: therefore, when you have played away the summer, and winter comes, you have nothing to live upon; and, while you are starving with cold and hunger, I have a good, warm house over my head, and plenty of provisions about me."

Gaiety and folly are all very well for the summer, but when the winter comes they change to discontent and wretchedness.

THE COUNTRYMAN AND THE SNAKE.

A Villager, in a frosty, snowy winter, found a Snake under a hedge, almost dead with cold. He could not help having a compassion for the poor creature, so he brought it home, and laid it upon the hearth near the fire; but it had not lain there long, before (being revived with the heat) it began to erect itself, and fly at his wife and children, filling the whole cottage with dreadful hissings. The Countrymen hearing an outcry, and perceiving what the matter was, caught up a mattock, and soon dispatched him; upbraiding him at the same time in these words:—" Is this, vile wretch, the reward you make to him that saved your life? Die as you deserve; but a single death is too good for you."

Kindness to the ungrateful and the vicious is goodness thrown away.

THE FOX AND THE SICK LION.

It was reported that the Lion was sick, and the beasts were made to believe that they could not make their court better than by going to visit him. Upon this they generally went; but it was particularly taken notice of that the Fox was not one of the number. The Lion, therefore dispatched one of his jackalls to sound him about it, and ask him why he had so little charity and respect as never to come near him at a time when he lay so dangerously ill, and everybody else had been to see him. "Why," replies the Fox, "pray present my duty to his majesty, and tell him that I have the same respect for him as ever, and have been coming several times to kiss his royal hand; but I am so terribly frightened at the mouth of his cave, to see the print of my fellow-subjects' feet all pointing forwards, and none backwards, that I have not resolution enough to venture in." Now the truth of the matter was, that this sickness of the Lion's was only a sham to draw the beasts into his den, the more easily to devour them.

It is never safe to trust the cruel.

INDEX.